Also By Liliana Rhodes

His Every Whim
His Every Whim, Part 1
His One Desire, Part 2
His Simple Wish, Part 3
His True Fortune, Part 4
The Billionaire's Whim - Boxed Set

Canyon Cove Billionaires
Playing Games
No Regrets
Second Chance

Made Man Trilogy
Soldier
Capo
Boss
Made Man Dante - Boxed Set

Made Man Novels
Made Man Sonny

The Crane Curse Trilogy
Charming the Alpha
Resisting the Alpha
Needing the Alpha
The Crane Curse Trilogy Boxed Set

Wolf at Her Door

Second Chance

A CANYON COVE NOVEL

Liliana Rhodes

Jaded Speck
PUBLISHING

Published by
Jaded Speck Publishing
5042 Wilshire Blvd #30861
Los Angeles, CA 90036

Second Chance
A Canyon Cove Novel
Copyright © 2015 by Liliana Rhodes
Cover by CT Cover Designs

ISBN 978-1-939918-16-1

This book is a work of fiction. The names, characters, places, and incidents are products of the writer's imagination or have been used fictitiously and are not to be construed as real. Any resemblance to persons, living or dead, actual events, locales or organizations is entirely coincidental.

All rights reserved. No part of this book may be reproduced, scanned, or distributed in any manner whatsoever without written permission from the author except in the case of brief quotation embodied in critical articles and reviews.

Dedication

To my son,
I love you.

Acknowledgements

First of all, I want to thank my readers who have always been so supportive and wonderful. I have the best readers! Seriously, I do.

I'd like to take this time to thank a few friends, in no particular order, who are always there for me when I'm tucked away in my writing cave--
- Kristina L. for all her help and motivation even when I have my moments of doubts,
- Donna H. who is always willing to drop everything to give me her opinion,
- Marian Tee for nudging my competitive side with her impressive word count,
- Malia Mallory and Clarise for always knowing the right things to say,
- and last but not least, my editor Wendy who puts up with my lateness and craziness.

To my dad who always asks about what I'm writing and tells me how proud he is of me. I love you, Dad.

And to my husband and my son who are always so patient when I'm writing.

Prologue

Six Months Ago

Tara

As Ashley Boone and I walked along the carpeted hall of Jefferson Manor, I couldn't help but think about home. Not the house I grew up in, but the elegance and mystery of the South. In some ways I felt all I had were my memories. But whenever I saw Ashley with her husband, billionaire Xander Boone, it reminded me of what I lost a long time ago.

But more than just being my boss's wife, Ashley was a good friend. She was pregnant with their first child and was excited to show me the baby's room. As she walked into the room, I noticed the faintest pregnant waddle as her dark wavy hair swung around her shoulders.

"This is a nice color," I said, admiring the paint. "What is it? Taupe?"

The room was jungle themed. Hanging on the wall was a quilt with a fuzzy baby monkey, elephant, and lion on it. In the corner was a brown microfiber rocking chair. Long blue curtains hung from the wide windows. The room was painted a nice taupe, just dark enough to be interesting.

Ashley shrugged. "I don't know the name of it. I brought them the quilt and asked them to make it the color of the monkey's butt." She patted the monkey on the wall hanging.

"Well, that's the best looking monkey butt I've ever seen. And trust me, I've dated a few monkey butts in my time," I said with a laugh.

"Is that why you never married?"

"It's complicated," I whispered, barely able to speak for a moment as I thought about Mason Abernathy. "There was one man. Ooh boy, was he ever a man!" I fanned myself dramatically and forced a smile onto my face. "The love of my life."

"What happened to him?"

"I wish I knew..." I said wistfully and slowly ran my hand over the fuzzy material of the wall hanging. Although he was never far from my thoughts, it had been a very long time since I spoke about Mason. "I didn't grow up rich, but my parents knew horses were all I cared about. For my eighteenth birthday, they scrimped and saved to buy me an old horse, my beloved Ladyfinger. She was a beauty. We didn't have land for her so she had to be kept at a ranch where I could rent a stall. I started working there to pay for her boarding. Ended up making it a career. Everything I do here to take care of the horses, I learned at Abernathy Ranch."

A lock of my sandy blonde hair fell into my eyes. I pushed it back and tightened my ponytail. Talking about Mason after all this time was bittersweet.

"Did your boyfriend work there, too? Is that how you met him?"

"Yes, he did. Mason's family owned the stables and the entire town. His family wanted him to learn the family horse business from the bottom up. Shovelin' shit and all. Chances are if you've got a horse, the Abernathy family has lineage in it."

"So what happened?" Ashley asked quietly.

I turned away and crossed my arms over my chest, hugging myself and rubbing the soft fabric of my long sleeved t-shirt as the heartache came back stronger.

"He left," I said with a shrug. "He went away. He left for a business opportunity in Germany and never came back." I felt my throat tighten, and I cleared it as my eyes misted over. I hated feeling so vulnerable and hurt after all this time, especially in front of someone else, no matter how close I felt to her. I let out a long sigh and pursed my lips. "Well, that's not entirely true. He came back eventually, just not to me. Not a day passes that I don't think about him though."

I was lucky that Ashley knew me well enough that she didn't ask anything else. Talking about Mason's leaving was the last thing I wanted to do.

***

A few days later, I was prepping a horse stall for a colt that was arriving in the morning. Entering the stable with an arm full of hay, my feet froze as I heard a trio of voices. Two of them I knew as Ashley and Xander, but the third I hadn't heard in fifteen years.

It can't be him.

His voice was deep and with his Southern drawl, I knew it could only be one person. I forced my eyes to focus on the man with Ashley and Xander, but the darkness of the stable made my eyes slow to adjust. Wishing my arms were empty, I rubbed my eyes into my shoulder as best as I could until my vision cleared.

Mason was taller than I remembered, but he still cut a striking figure in his grey suit and black cowboy boots. His hair was turning grey, but still had enough of the brown I remembered running my fingers through. I blinked quickly, trying to clear my vision of Mason and see who was really standing there, but nothing changed. It was him.

He patted a colt on the neck and my thoughts rushed. *Was it an Abernathy colt we were getting? No, I would've remembered if it was. So why is he here?*

As he stepped out of the colt's stall, he squinted at the sun behind me as he pulled a handkerchief out of his pocket and wiped his hands.

"Am I seeing an angel?" he whispered.

"I knew I recognized your voice," Tara said. "How funny that after all this time I didn't need to see you to know it was you."

My feet had a mind of their own and moved me closer to him. I tried to act normal, but I didn't know what normal was anymore. I never thought I would see him again.

Mason met me halfway. I looked up into his eyes and the years vanished. All the feelings I had locked away for so long had returned. I felt like the twenty-two year old I was when we dated and not the woman in her thirties seeing the man she had dreamed about for fifteen years.

As I soaked Mason in, he smiled, but his dimples were hidden by his short beard that was grey where it covered his chin. I was happy to see his face looked a little weathered from the sun. It meant he wasn't sitting behind a desk like I remembered his father did.

"Your hair. It's lighter," Mason said, his voice a mix of awe and confusion.

"And your face is older," I said as I laughed. "It's been a long time, Mason."

"Too long."

His husky voice pierced my heart and reminded me of the pain he caused.

"And whose fault is that?" I blurted out.

"What do you mean?"

"Never mind," I mumbled, shaking my head and looking down at my boots. "It's not something I care to relive right now."

"Let me take you to dinner. Let's catch up and talk about old times. Or not. Whatever you want. Just give me a little of your time," he said.

"I think I can manage that. Come get me in an hour. I'm a busy woman, you know," I said with a grin.

I dropped the hay into the colt's stall and looked the horse over as my mind spun. An hour? What was I thinking? I didn't have enough time to get ready in an hour.

As they walked out of the barn, I busied myself with the young horse, but my eyes kept darting over to Mason. After a few minutes, Maya, my niece, entered the stable and rushed over.

Maya's dark blonde hair was the same color as mine at her age before I started coloring it. She wore it pulled back from her face, and it fell down her back in long springy curls. Maya had inherited all of her looks from my sister Brooke, even the Murphy family curves and our short stature. The only thing that made her different were her bright green eyes.

"He's early! Oh, he's beautiful," she said as she filled a bucket of water.

"Can you keep an eye on him? I have some things I need to take care of," I said, hoping she wouldn't ask any questions.

"No problem. I told you, while I'm here, I'm here to help. I had nowhere else to go and you took me in."

"You're being dramatic," I said as I patted her shoulder. "You're just going through a rough patch. Happens to us all."

"I mean it though. You've been a lifesaver."

I felt like time was racing and as much as I wanted to stay and talk, I had to get going if I was going to have enough time to get ready for Mason.

"This is an Abernathy colt, so I'm sure he'll have no problem adjusting. But if you need me for anything, just text me," I said as I left the stall.

I picked up my pace as I stepped out of the stable, but Mason surprised me. He slipped his arm around my waist and pulled me close to him.

"I couldn't help but notice there isn't a ring on your finger," he said, his voice grave.

"What are you doing?"

Surprise filled my voice. Even though I really wanted to stay in his arms, I pushed my hands against his strong chest to give myself space. I had to remember how much he hurt me before. I wouldn't let that happen again.

"Isn't it obvious? I'm going to kiss you."

His head lowered towards mine and I pushed him further away.

"No! Just no. Who do you think you are? Am I supposed to just drop every ounce of sanity because you want to kiss me? It's been fifteen years, Mason. You don't know anything about me anymore," I said.

"I know you, Tara. The time away doesn't change anything between us. At least it doesn't for me."

"Time changes everything. Things ended when you left. Just because you're here now doesn't mean things will go back to the way they were."

"Are you dating anyone? Are you married?" He barked his questions at me. I hated having to admit the truth.

"No," I said, my voice full of frustration.

"Then why can't we pretend we were never apart? We're not kids anymore, Tara. We don't need the foreplay of playing coy. You can't tell me you feel differently now than you did back then. I can see it in how you look at me."

"Forget about how I look at you. That doesn't matter. And forget about dinner tonight."

"What do you mean forget about it?"

His tone was demanding, and it made me push back even more. Inside though, I was struggling. The naive girl he left fifteen years ago was gone. I was stronger now except for my knees. He still made them weak.

"I don't think I want to see you right now. I don't know if I ever want to see you," I said. "I told you, I've changed and you need to accept that. Just as I'm seeing that you've changed, too. And not for the better."

I pushed further away from him, finally breaking his hold on me, and stormed down the dusty path to my cottage. I was glad I didn't hear his footsteps behind me. I wasn't one of those women who wanted to be chased and followed. I needed to be alone.

Slamming the door behind me, I walked aimlessly into my home. Tears stung my eyes, but I refused to let them fall. I had cried too many times for that man.

How dare he grab me and try kissing me! I should have slapped him or kneed him in the balls, but I really wanted that kiss. I had been dreaming about his lips, his arms, everything about him for all these years.

Why did I push him away? I don't know. Something just didn't feel right. I wasn't that girl from all those years ago, I was different. I had changed and I wanted him to acknowledge that and see me for who I was now. But, deep down, I still wished he kissed me.

Mason

How dare she. I got into my car and sped away from Jefferson Manor as quickly as I could. As I drove back to the downtown area of Canyon Cove, I replayed my interaction with Tara in my head. I was trying to make sense of it, but it only fueled my anger more.

I pulled the car up to the hotel valet and took the ticket from him without saying a word. I didn't need to say anything; he knew who I was. Everyone did.

The heels of my boots clapped against the marble floor as I walked through the hotel lobby towards the bar. The last thing I wanted at that moment was to be alone with my thoughts in my suite. I knew all I would think about was her. She was all I had thought about for the past fifteen years. Being spurned by her wouldn't change that.

As I entered the bar, I found a small booth in a quiet corner. The bartender nodded in my direction and I raised two fingers at him. As I loosened my tie, he set a glass on the small table in front of me. In his other hand, he held a bottle.

"Good?" he asked as he held out the bottle.

I nodded and he poured my two fingers' worth. "Leave the bottle," I grunted.

As I took a sip, the bouquet of cheap perfume enveloped me. A young woman with sun-kissed blonde waves and a seductive pout slid across from me. She was pretty, but she wasn't Tara.

Seeing Tara was like stepping back in time for me. Every emotion rushed back as if only fifteen minutes had gone by instead of years. I should've kissed her. It had been on my mind for too long to not do it.

"Are you waiting for someone?" the woman asked nervously.

"Maybe," I said, thinking about Tara.

"It's a woman, isn't it? Maybe I can help you forget."

While I knew what she meant, there was something about her demeanor that told another story. She seemed lost, like a helpless kitten. I was curious about her story.

I looked over towards the bartender and raised my glass to him. He nodded and brought over an empty glass and set it on the table.

"It's always about a woman," I said as I poured her a drink then slid it over to her.

"No, thank you," she said, pushing the glass away. "I don't drink while—"

She cut herself off, and her eyes drifted towards another booth where a man wearing sunglasses sat.

"Not while you're on a job." I finished for her. "What's your name?" I asked.

"Candi. Of course I know yours, but I can call you whatever you'd like."

"Mason is fine. How much for him to go away?"

I darted my eyes towards her pimp then back at her. She chewed her lip nervously then lowered her voice.

"He never goes away."

"But he won't follow you to a room," I said.

She nodded. I pulled my wallet out and slid a small wad of hundreds across the table to her.

"Let's go."

I held my hand out to her and helped her out of the seat. Her hands felt dry, like someone who spent her day cleaning, not like the high-priced escort she was pretending to be. As we walked out of the bar, I felt her tremble.

The harsh lights of the elevator revealed how thin and withdrawn she was. Her eyes were slightly hallowed and her skin was sickly pale. She reminded me of a worn doll that someone had dressed up, hoping to make it look nicer.

As the elevator rose to the penthouse suites, she stared out the glass at the lights below. She hugged herself and rubbed her thin arms. I took my jacket off and placed it over her shoulders.

"Thank you, Mr. Abernathy," she said as she turned to face me.

"I told you before, it's Mason. Now what's your name?"

"Candi."

"Your real name."

Her eyes darted away from me and she looked out again.

"He's not here."

"Tricia," she whispered.

The doors opened and I led her down the hall to my suite. Housekeeping had left the lights on and music playing from my call to the hotel earlier. A large bouquet of deep red roses sat on a vase on the table.

Tricia gawked as she entered the room. While she admired the roses, I picked up the room phone and called down to the lobby.

"Good evening, Mr. Abernathy. Is there something I can help you with?"

"Connect me with Security, please."

"Right away, sir."

After a brief wait, a man's familiar voice came on the line.

"Mr. Abernathy? This is Joseph, head of security."

"Good, I was hoping you were on duty," I said. I turned away from Tricia and lowered my voice. "There's a man in the bar wearing sunglasses."

"Yes, I saw him arrive earlier with a young woman."

"She's with me now. Take care of him. Scare the living shit out of him. I don't want him bothering this young lady or any others again."

I hung up the phone and walked over to Tricia, who was sitting on the couch looking uncomfortable. She smiled sweetly at me and pushed her small chest forward in what I guessed she thought was a sexy pose.

"I'm ready when you are," she said.

"Why were you here with that scum?"

"What? Oh, you mean in the bar? Let's not talk about that. Let's talk about how I can make you feel better."

"I'll cut to the chase, Tricia," I said as I perched myself on the arm of the chair across from her. "I live in hotels. I haven't had a place to call home in fifteen years. I see girls like you all the time, and every once in a while I bring one up to my room like I did with you. Right now, you have a choice to make. You either tell me what you're doing with him, or you go back down and take a chance with another John."

As she looked around the suite, I saw her eyes stop every so often as she took everything in. Her eyes settled back on me. She took a deep breath before speaking.

"If we're being honest, you seem like a pretty straight up guy. And you gave me more money than I've ever seen. Most men would've started grabbing at me in the elevator."

"I didn't bring you up here for that."

"Then why am I here?"

"To give you a chance. Listen, I've had a rough day. Tell me why you're with that asshole and I'll see what I can do to help you."

"Only if you tell me about her," she said, reaching over to touch my knee.

My eyes met hers and after our silent conversation, I knew I didn't have to play dumb. She read me like an open book.

"You first," I said.

"Maybe I do need that drink."

"We both do." In the freezer, I kept a bottle of Grey Goose that I pulled out and poured into a couple of glasses. "You look like you haven't eaten in days. Order whatever you want from room service."

"Anything?"

Before I could finish nodding, she grabbed the phone and pressed the button. As I set the glasses down on an end table, I heard her order enough to feed an army.

"There's no way you can eat that much," I said. I didn't need her to answer, I had done this enough times before to know her story without hearing it. She wanted to bring the leftovers home.

She grinned and looked like a child, which angered me even more. I hoped Joseph would use his fists to get his point across on that lowlife.

"Thank you," she whispered as she hung up the phone. "That man, Mr. Dunham, owns the building we live in. My father is a gambler, just not a very good one. He's done what he could for us, but the best he could do was this apartment in the South End. When we couldn't pay the rent, Mr. Dunham made me an offer." Tears welled in her eyes. "I didn't know any other way out. I've been working seven days a week wherever people will hire me, but it's never enough. I'm the oldest of five and most of them are still in school, so they can't help."

I put my hand up to tell her to stop talking. I didn't mean to make her cry. I found a box of tissues and handed it to her.

"How old are you?"

"Twenty-two. I should be in college or out on my own, but I can't leave my brothers and sisters like that," she sniffled.

"We have to get your family out of there."

"We don't have any place to go."

"Call them. Tell them to pack whatever means the most to them and that a car will pick them up later. You'll stay here for a few days until I find a home where all of you can live."

"But we can't afford anything," she cried.

"You don't have to worry about that anymore."

"But then..." her voice trailed off and she looked down, afraid to ask her next question. "What do you want from me?"

"I'm opening an office in Canyon Cove. I need someone who lives here to run it. Someone I can trust." Her gaze met mine again and I saw confusion spread across her face. "You've managed a household with four children and a gambling father. You've offered yourself in order to keep a roof over their head when you could have left them. I can't train integrity like that."

"But--"

"I'm not done. I'll arrange for a house for your family to live in. A small deduction will come out of your salary to pay for it. In exchange, I expect you to manage my office here. What do you say?"

She eyed me suspiciously as she took a sip of her drink. "Tell me about her first."

She surprised me. It made me feel that much better about my offer.

"Her name is Tara," I said, leaning back in the chair. "I was going to propose to her tonight, but she didn't want to see me."

"What did you do?" she said, her voice full of accusation.

"I didn't do anything. All I did was try kissing her."

"You're leaving something out." Her eyes narrowed.

"It's nothing really, but the last time we saw each other was fifteen years ago. She thinks I don't know her anymore, but I do. I always have. I know her better than I know myself."

"How can you? Have you been spying on her?"

I laughed. "No, of course not. Today was a chance meeting. Fate finally stepped in and brought us back together. I don't want to go any longer without her."

Now it was Tricia's turn to laugh. "You're an idiot, you know that? You can't expect things to just go back where you left off. You need to woo her. Women want foreplay, and not just with sex, but with relationships too. Trust me on that."

I was shocked that she felt so comfortable speaking to me like this. People rarely had the balls to talk back to me or tell me I was wrong.

"I think you and I will work well together," I said.

"You really meant everything you said? About my family and the house? The job?"

"I don't bullshit people. I meant every word."

"Then I'll take the job." She stuck her hand out to me to shake, but then pulled it back at the last second. "But only on one condition."

"What is it?"

"You let me help you get your girl back."

I grabbed her hand and we shook. "It's a deal."

Tara

I was cleaning up around the cottage when I heard a soft knock on the door. The cottage was on the Boone's property, not far from the main house. I could live wherever I wanted, but the small house had a coziness I adored so when they offered it to me to live, I accepted.

I didn't need to look to see who was knocking. It could only be one of two people, Maya or Ashley. As I opened the door, Ashley started talking immediately.

"So tell me about this guy you call the love of your life," Ashley said with a smile as she walked in.

"Well hello to you too," I said. "Can't we talk about something else?"

"No, I've never seen you light up the way you did when you said his name. Everything about you changed. You have to tell me. I won't take no for an answer."

"You know, Xander is right. You are stubborn."

"I've never said any differently. Now spill it."

She tapped the table with an impatient look. I knew she wouldn't let it drop just like I knew what her reaction would be.

"Mason was my first love, my first heartbreak, my first, well, not everything, but he made it feel like that."

"Go on," she said as she leaned forward and rested her chin on her hands.

"I don't know what to say."

"Everything, Tara. Every single detail. I'm your friend, you're supposed to tell me all the sordid details."

"Well, I don't know about sordid, but we did have a lot of fun," I said with a laugh. "Honestly, I can't even tell you what it was about him. I mean I remember vividly the first day I saw him, what he was wearing, how I reacted to him. I think I remember feelings more than anything. He made me feel special and beautiful. I never felt like I had to be anyone other than myself with him. We were only together about eight months, but there was something about it that felt like it would never end, in a good way."

"So what happened?" she asked.

"It ended."

Ashley shot me a dirty look that made me burst out laughing.

"Okay, okay, I'll tell you everything. He left the ranch and took my heart with him. He had an invitation to go to Germany to learn more about some environmental something or other. He was only supposed to be gone for a few months, but he never came back. I never heard from him again."

"Never? He just disappeared?"

"Well, he didn't come back like he said he would, and he never called. I never heard from him while I was still down there and eventually I just couldn't stay there anymore, so I left."

It didn't feel like it was me telling the story. I had lived through it so many times that I was numb. The slightest thing reminded me of Mason and when it did, I felt like I was taken back in time.

"You must have tried looking him up. Do you know what happened to him?"

"I've searched for him online but never really found much. Just mostly his business stuff like how he took over running Abernathy Ranch like his father always wanted him to. I've never found anything personal, not even a photo of him. I don't know where he lives, if he ever got married, nothing. Sometimes I feel like he never existed. Anyway, it doesn't matter."

"What do you mean? Why not? He's here. You just saw him."

"And he asked me out on a date and then he kissed me so I cancelled it."

"You did what? I thought you were excited to see him again."

"I was, but everything felt too much like it did in the past."

"But isn't that good? You said you were crazy in love."

"I was. And maybe I still am. But it's not right. It was so long ago and we're different people. I've changed and he has to see that."

"I think there's more to it than just that," she said.

I thought about what happened when I pushed him away. The ache that had been there since he left came back and reminded me what felt wrong.

"I need to know what happened. I need him to tell me why he didn't call, why he didn't look for me." I pushed aside my hurt and anger replaced it.

"I waited for him and he didn't care enough to even call. I deserve better than that."

Part One

A Chance to Remember

Chapter One

Tara

Present Day
October

Ashley and I were seated in Mirabella's, the restaurant and pastry shop we met at for just about everything. The warm colors of the restaurant were accented with pumpkins, ghosts, and goblins for the upcoming holiday.

"I still can't believe you cancelled on Mason at the last minute again," Ashley said.

"You ever have that one guy you've never been able to stop thinking about?" I glanced over at Ashley as she sipped her coffee. She didn't need to answer. "No, of course not, Xander was the one and only for you."

"Excuse me?" Ashley said with a laugh. "We weren't always together."

"You had what? Weeks apart? I'm talking years, honey." I shook my head. "For years, Mason has been on my mind like a song you can't get out of your head, but worse." I chuckled as I vainly tried to push away my sadness. "There was no one else like him back home in North Carolina or any other place else. Trust me, I've looked."

"So then it's good you're going on that date with him."

"No, it's not," I said as I lifted my hot chocolate to my lips.

The waitress came by and put down a plate of pastries between Ashley and I. I wanted one, but I couldn't muster up the energy to reach for it. Everything was focused on remembering him.

"Then why not? How could it be a bad thing when you've been thinking about him for all this time?"

"Ashley, I've been thrown from a horse, kicked by a bucking stallion, but nothing in my life has hurt me more than Mason's leaving. He might as well have ripped my beating heart out of my chest when he didn't come back."

"When did that happen?"

I sighed. "Fifteen years ago. It's hard to believe it's been so long since I last saw him. I still feel that pain as if it happened yesterday."

I wrapped my fingers around the mug so the ceramic would warm them. With a soft laugh, I looked back at Ashley.

"Everything reminds me of him," I said. "It always has. Even something as insignificant as this hot chocolate makes my mind drift over to him. All my memories of Mason are right here," I said as I put my hand over my heart. "I can even remember the first time I ever saw him and feel that excitement as if it just happened."

"Was it love at first sight?"

Ashley rested her chin on her hand, her eyes wide as she waited for my answer.

"No, it was anything but love," I said with a laugh. "I hated him. And the fact that he was such a gorgeous man made me want to hate him even more."

Fifteen Years Ago

"What do you mean I didn't get the job?" I asked. "It's still March, I thought they were announcing it at the beginning of April."

Maddie Maguire and I were in the tack room cleaning up after a day of training. Her long brown ponytail swung as she shook her head.

"I heard old man Abernathy's son is coming back home," she said. "He wants him to learn the business from the ground up so instead of getting someone who deserves the job a chance, that Mason is getting the job."

"Well, I'll be damned if I'm just gonna stand here and take that. I've worked my ass off the past four years here in the hopes that I would get that job. I need that job."

"What are you going to do?"

"I'm going to march right into that big house and give them a piece of my mind. They have no right to do this."

"Listen, Tara, I know things have been hard at home since your dad had that heart attack, but you can't just go in there and think that they will let you stay here if you go off on them like that."

I shook my head as frustration consumed me. I couldn't just stand there and let them give the job that I had worked so hard for to someone who didn't deserve it.

Maddie's brow was wrinkled with concern. She knew how short-tempered I was and she knew how bad things were at home. I needed this job to help support my family, but I needed to stand up for myself first and foremost.

"I promise I won't lose it, but I need to go in there. I need to understand why I didn't get the job and why they're just handing it over to his son. Old man Abernathy is a reasonable man, I can't believe he would just do this."

"Have you ever been into the big house?" she asked.

"No, why?"

"Because you'll never see anything else like it. The first time I went in there, I was overwhelmed."

"Please, you know shit like that doesn't bother me. It's just money."

"Not like this. Money doesn't even begin to describe this."

Maddie had a tendency to exaggerate at times, and I was sure this was one of those times. I could care less how much money the Abernathys had or how big their house was.

I hung up the final bridle and walked out of the tack room and through the barn without looking back. Even though it was the end of our work day, I knew Maddie well enough to know that she would wait around for me.

It had been four years since I first entered the gates of Abernathy Ranch, but this would be the first time I entered the main house. I followed the winding walkway through the field separating the barns and the stables to the main house.

Although I had seen the house hundreds of times, it had never looked as large as it did at that moment. I was suddenly very aware of my worn jeans, my blonde hair pulled back into a messy ponytail, and the dirt under my fingernails after a long day of working with horses.

Abernathy Manor was a huge two-story stone mansion with tall, wood-framed gables. After the original house was destroyed in a fire fifty years ago, a new house was built years later on the remains of the original structure along with a nearby barn.

The mansion was a never-ending work in progress as Mrs. Abernathy continued to change and fix things in the house. She even added stained glass that she had collected on her trips to Italy. The result was that Abernathy Manor was an impressive combination between the old and the new.

Breathing in deep as I approached the house, I decided to follow the stone walkway around to the front. While no one had ever said so, it was common knowledge that anyone who worked at Abernathy Ranch was only welcomed in the house if they were invited.

While I knew Maddie would have opted for one of the back doors, there was no way I was going to lower myself to that. If I was going to make a fuss about not getting the job, then I was going to do it in the front door, not the back.

As I approached the large wooden double doors with panels of stained glass, I tried to see if I could peek in, but I couldn't see anything. I listened as the doorbell chimed through the house and was happy to see Lucy, Maddie's sister, open the door.

Lucy had her dark hair pulled back into a tight bun. She wore the crisp grey uniform all Abernathy house employees wore. Maddie and Lucy had spent most of their lives at the ranch since their mother worked there when they were children. Since she didn't always have sitters, she brought the girls to work with her. Once they were old enough, they started working there too.

"Tara! What are you doing here?" she whispered as she stepped outside and closed the door behind her.

"I'm here to talk to old man Abernathy. I heard he's giving the manager job to his son. So I'm here to give him a piece of my mind."

"Well then, come in I guess. He's in the study with Mrs. Abernathy and Mason."

Lucy opened the door wide, and for the first time I got a glimpse at the inside of Abernathy Manor. As I stepped past the doorway, my eyes were drawn to the glass wall ahead of me. On the other side of the glass was an open courtyard framed by balconies from the second floor of the house. In the courtyard was a lush garden with a seating area and a fountain. I had never seen anything like it inside a house.

"This is your first time here, isn't it?" Lucy asked, but didn't wait for me to answer. "You have to see this." She opened a small panel in the wall by the door and pressed something. With a gentle whir, the glass wall slowly slid open as the panels disappeared.

"Holy shit," I said under my breath.

"I love that. Trust me when I say you don't want to be the person who left it open when it starts raining." She tapped the button again and the glass began moving in the opposite direction, closing the wall. "Come this way, I'll take you to Mr. Abernathy's study."

I finally understood why Maddie warned that the house was overwhelming. Everywhere I looked there was something that caught my eye and made me forget why I was there. Not only that, but the obvious wealth in the house made me feel out of place. The home I lived in with my parents could easily fit into that courtyard with room to spare. The thought reminded me why I was there and even though it made me angry, I focused on that and not the lavishness of Abernathy Manor.

"That's his study over there with the double doors," Lucy said. "I'd love to stick around, but I need to check on dinner."

Lucy ran off down the hall before I could say anything. I pushed my shoulders back and held my head up high as I walked towards the large double doors. As I approached, I heard raised voices coming from the other side. I recognized Mrs. Abernathy's and her husband's voices immediately. There was one more voice I didn't know, but that only left one person—their spoiled son, Mason.

"No," Mrs. Abernathy said. "You've been away for six years now, first with college and then graduate school. Not once did you come home in all that time. I am not letting you spend another year away, especially not all the way in Germany."

"I wasn't asking for permission, Mother. I was telling you that I'm going," Mason said.

"Mason, you know your father isn't well and—"

"Do not talk about me like I'm not here," Mr. Abernathy said. "Now Mason, as my son, you know I'm expecting you to take care of everything here once I'm gone."

"Dad, don't start."

"It's the truth. I can't sit here and pretend I'm immortal." Mr. Abernathy laughed. "You're twenty-four years old and you'll do whatever you want to do. I'm glad I raised you to be your own man. But my time is limited, so I'm asking you to take some time to work here. I need you to learn the business. I need to know that you can take care of it once I'm gone."

In the four years that I had been working there, old man Abernathy lived up to what we called him. We didn't mean any disrespect, it was just our way of letting off steam from working for someone we rarely saw. None of us knew exactly how old Mr. Abernathy was, but he was frail and gaunt and looked like his wife's father instead of her husband. Considering he rebuilt Abernathy Manor more than forty years ago, we knew he had to be up there.

The voices in the study had calmed down, but instead of knocking to tell them I was there, I leaned closer to one of the doors and pressed my ear against it. The door swung open, knocking me off balance, but instead of falling I was caught by a pair of muscular arms.

I looked up to see who the arms belonged to and saw a rugged, tanned face smiling at me. He had a closely cropped beard, short dark hair, and warm light brown eyes. As he helped set me onto my feet his smile grew, revealing dimples.

"You should watch where you're going, sweetheart. I might not always be around to catch you," he said.

My breath caught in my throat and my blood rushed to my cheeks. I couldn't believe how gorgeous and cocky this man was. My initial reaction was to flirt back with him, but then I realized who he was—Mason Abernathy, the reason I had to continue working my ass off.

"My name isn't sweetheart and the last thing I need is for you to catch me," I said.

"If you say so, but that's not how it looked to me," Mason said as he walked past.

"Asshole," I muttered.

Mrs. Abernathy was an overly thin woman with silvery grey short hair and a pointed nose that turned up slightly at the tip. She eyed me up and down with her eyebrows raised and disdain covering her face.

"I didn't hear anyone announce you. Do they just let anyone in nowadays?" she said as she turned towards her husband.

"Iris, can you please give us a moment?" Mr. Abernathy said. "I think I know what this is about."

Her lips curled as she walked past me and out the door. Mr. Abernathy sat behind an oversized desk that would have dwarfed most rooms, but was almost lost in this one. He was a slight man with wispy grey hair and glasses. Whenever I saw him he wore a perfectly tailored suit, and today was no exception. Behind him were floor to ceiling bookshelves, and for a moment I forgot again why I was there as I tried to read some of the titles.

"I'm sorry to barge in on you, Sir," I said.

"No, Tara, you should have heard the news from me and not from the rumor mill. This is my fault. Please sit down." He cleared his throat and drummed his fingers on the desk as I sat in an oversized chair facing the desk. "I'll be honest with you, but I'm sure this won't make you feel any better. Until Mason returned, I had planned to give you the manager job."

"Then why not just let me have it?"

He sighed. "He's my son, and one day all of this will be his. He needs to learn the ropes whether he wants to or not," he muttered. "I need your help though. I need you to show him the ropes."

"You've got to be kidding me," I said as I stood up. "No, there's no way I'm going to help him with the job that should have been mine."

"You're a hard worker, Tara. Mason isn't going to stay here for good. I know him. He'll be here a couple of months tops and then he'll be gone again. Just be patient. The job will be yours once he's gone."

I sat back down and steadily met his gaze. I loved working at the ranch and he knew it. He also knew I was supporting my family at home. Mr. Abernathy had always been a fair man, but the thought of having to work alongside that cocky, beautiful man that was his son pissed me off. I wasn't going to do something stupid though.

"Okay, I'll do it," I said.

Present Day

Ashley laughed. "You didn't hate him."

"I did," I said, holding back my laughter. "He was so perfect and confident, nothing like me. I couldn't stand him."

"Then how did you two end up together?" Ashley's phone lit up and buzzed on top of the table. "Just a second, it's Xander," she said as she brought the phone up to her ear.

I left the table to give her some privacy and made my way to the cash register at the front of the cafe. The manager, a petite blonde with a kind face, smiled at me.

"Hi Amy, I'll take care of our check," I said.

"It's already taken care of," she said.

"What do you mean?" I looked back at the table where Ashley was juggling her phone while digging in her purse for her wallet.

She widened her brown eyes as they met mine and then her eyes darted towards the door. I followed her gaze to the glass doors and spotted Mason standing outside.

Dammit! I can't believe he's here.

"He made me promise to not tell you he's waiting for you," Amy said. "I hope that was alright."

"It's fine," I said, letting out a deep sigh. "I have to deal with him eventually."

Ashley put her phone away, took one last sip of her water, and joined me at the register with her wallet in hand.

"Please don't tell me you paid," she said.

"I didn't get to. Looks like Mason tracked me down."

Ashley looked past me and smiled. "He's just waiting there for you," she said.

"He got here shortly after you did," Amy said. "He's been standing there for over an hour."

I shook my head. "Crazy sonofabitch," I said. "You asked how we ended up together? That's exactly how." I pointed at him then turned back towards Ashley and Amy. "He's stubborn. He doesn't take no for an answer. He always gets what he wants. He's demanding and infuriatingly handsome."

"You're going to go out to dinner with him, aren't you?" Ashley asked.

"I don't think I have a choice."

"I don't think you want a choice. You still love him, don't you?"

I nodded my head slowly. "I never stopped."

Chapter Two

Tara

As I pushed the door open, Mason turned around and opened it further. He smiled at me, making soft wrinkles at the corners of his eyes and exposing his dimples. My heart did that annoying lurch it always did whenever I saw him, making me gasp slightly for air.

I smiled back at him as I took a deep breath. Seeing him again was like taking a step back in time. Only this time I promised myself I wouldn't give him my heart. It still hurt from the last time he had it.

"I'll see you tomorrow, Ashley," I said as I turned to hug her.

She hugged me back tightly. "I'm expecting details," she whispered before letting go.

As she got into her car, I turned towards Mason and his piercing gaze.

"Stop looking at me like that," I said. "You know I've always hated that."

"I have a lot of time to make up for. And I know you, you're going to make this hard on me."

"You deserve it to be hard on you."

"That's debatable," he said as his hand touched my lower back. "I'll drive you home."

"Who said I needed a ride?"

"I know Ashley was your ride. How do you think I got here?"

We walked to his car, a black Tesla, a fancy electric car I had seen recently in a magazine. It was just like Mason to be more concerned about the environment than wasting his money on something extravagant.

"Have you been following me?" I asked with a laugh.

"Some would call it stalking," he said, his dimples deepened as he grinned.

"You're really something else, you know that?"

"I do. It's why you've never forgotten about me."

"I definitely didn't forget how cocky you are."

"Tara, it's been fifteen years and you still look at me the same way you did all that time ago."

"Maybe you're seeing things."

"Maybe I am. Or maybe I'm seeing what I know you see in me. I know how I look at you. It's the same way I've always looked at you."

"Like a starved wolf." I laughed nervously. *Why was he being so serious? What was going on?*

"If I'm starved, it's because I'm only hungry for you. You're the only one who has ever made me feel this way. Ever."

They were the words I had dreamed about hearing, but I wasn't ready for them. My heart fluttered in my chest with a mixture of happiness and pain. I didn't know what his words meant. *Was he serious?*

"I'm not ready for this," I said as I looked out the window of the moving car.

"What do you mean? I've spent all this time thinking about you, hoping that one day fate would bring us together again, and it has."

"We just got back together. Wait, what am I saying? We're not even together. This is the first time we've seen each other in months."

He had me so confused I didn't know what I was saying or thinking anymore.

"I'm tired of wasting time, Tara," he said as he pulled the car over. He turned to face me, and his eyes were intense and his jaw was set. "I am taking you out to dinner tomorrow night. I will not take no for an answer."

"But--"

"No buts. It's just dinner. If what I think is still there between us, then maybe it'll be something more. If I'm wrong, at least we'll get a nice meal out of it." He turned the car back onto the road, then stole a glance at me. "Go ahead, say it."

"You're still the same cocky sonofabitch, aren't you?" I asked, barely hiding my smile.

He laughed softly. "The same son of a bitch you fell in love with. The one who hopes you might still feel the same way."

It was funny how long ago the time felt, but my feelings made me feel like everything just happened yesterday. It was all right on the surface waiting as if something deep down said that one day we would meet again. One day I'd feel everything for him anew. What I never expected was that fifteen years after we first met, he would be the same man who once swept me off my feet.

Fifteen Years Ago

I arrived at the ranch early in the morning. Today was Mason Abernathy's first day and as much as I had heard how he had worked the ranch before, I didn't expect much hard labor from that entitled jerk.

My stomach dropped as I approached the main stable and saw that the doors were wide open. I remembered locking up before I left the night before, but what if there was a break in? Each of those horses was worth more than I'd probably make in my life.

As I ran into the stable, Mason exited one of the stalls near the entry. My boots slipped on some hay. I was moving too fast to gain my footing on the wood floor when his arms wrapped around me.

"So far so good," he said, holding me close as his mouth spread into a smile. "Seems I am always around to catch you."

"Let me go," I said as I pushed him away.

"Until next time." He raised his eyebrows and grinned.

I stepped back from him and tried to collect myself, but my damn heart kept pounding whenever I thought about his catching me.

Maybe I need to slip on some hay again.

I shook my head to get the thought out of my mind and finally noticed how Mason filled out his jeans. He was wearing an ivory t-shirt that was a little damp from sweat, making it cling to his muscular chest.

Maybe I need a roll in the hay.

I looked around the stable, trying to get my mind off of undressing my new boss, and mentally counted the horses. They were quiet as they ate.

"You're here early," I said, forcing myself to not end my sentence with a question mark.

"I like taking care of them before the heat of the day becomes too much."

"You didn't have to do this. You're the manager, I would've taken care of it."

"That's not how I work," he said. "Listen, I can only imagine what you think of me. I've been called a cocky bastard, a spoiled handsome asshole, and I'm sure that's exactly what you think of me."

Despite not wanting to react, I found myself nodding.

"See, I know. And I don't mind it, I am a cocky bastard. And handsome." He smiled and his dimples made another appearance. "Remember you agreed to that too."

"I did not!"

"You did. And I have all these horses as my witnesses." He took his cowboy hat off the hook and put it on. "Let's go for a ride. I'm not taking no for an answer."

His eyes were warm and trusting and despite how much I wanted to continue disliking him, he was winning me over.

"Okay, but you have to let me lead," I said.

"Not a problem, I'll be enjoying the view."

He wiggled his brow at me then walked out of the stable towards the round pen. Inside the pen was a young man I hadn't seen before. He was tall with dark wavy hair and as he cleaned, it was obvious he had done this before.

"Rafa, get the two horses." Mason called to him.

"Who's he?" I asked, keeping an eye on the boy as he entered the stable.

"Part time help. He's the real reason I came home."

"He's a little young. Is he yours?" I asked, surprised.

Mason laughed. "No. His sister is a good friend of mine and asked me to help him out. He's been getting into a bit of trouble lately."

Rafa led two horses to us and Mason took their reins. I climbed onto one of the horses and trotted down the path that led to the hills surrounding the ranch. Mason rode alongside me when the path was wide enough and slipped behind when it narrowed.

The ride was just what I needed to clear my mind. I breathed in the fresh air and decided to put aside any of my hard feelings about Mason getting the job over me.

We rode in silence, just taking in the rolling hills and the dark green leaves of the trees. As we approached a clearing, Mason went ahead and dismounted before taking the reins of my horse and helping me down.

"We need to talk," he said. "My father didn't handle this as well as he should have."

With the horses grazing, Mason and I looked across the valley as the sun made its way further into the sky.

"He wants you to learn the business," I said, thinking about my conversation with him.

"I don't need to manage a stable of horses to learn the business. I grew up here, it's already part of my life and not something I'm interested in taking over."

"But what about your dad? He said he's dying. I think that's why this is so important to him."

"My father has been dying most of my life," he scoffed. "Don't get me wrong, I love my father, but I always wanted a life outside of the ranch."

"Is that why you've been away so long?"

"You heard about that? Nice to know people talk about me."

"I...umm...we weren't talking about you," I said, stammering as he laughed.

"I've known Lucy and Maddie for years. If they weren't talking about me, they were talking about someone."

"My lips are sealed."

He touched my cheek and his thumb grazed my lips. This wasn't how I wanted our first day of working together to end up, but all I could think about was him kissing me.

"I'm only going to be here a couple of months," he said, turning towards the view.

"A couple months?" Are you going back to school?"

"No, I'm done. I just completed my Masters in Environmental Science at Yale and started my own environmental consulting firm. I haven't been home in years, but Chloe asked me to come home and help with Rafa. He's seventeen and getting in with the wrong crowd. He knows horses, so I figured some hard work would do him good. Once he's settled in here, I'm heading to Germany for a business opportunity. In other words, I'll be out of your way before you know it."

"Oh well, maybe you're not as bad as I thought."

"I'm not all suits and hundred dollar bills, if that's what you were thinking," he said. "As a matter of fact, I'm going to take you out to dinner sometime to prove that."

I studied his handsome face for a moment. As I opened my mouth to accept, something Maddie said a while back flitted through my mind.

"What for?" I asked. "So you can have your fun while you're here and then go?"

As I glared at him, he met my gaze steadily before cracking a smile.

"You can't fault a guy for trying. You're the prettiest thing I've seen around here in a long time. You keep this up and I promise one day I'll marry you."

I rolled my eyes. *Like that would happen.*

"You don't even know me," I said. "I think we should get back to work."

As I turned towards the horses, Mason reached out for my arm. The heel of my boot caught on a jagged rock and I tripped forward.

Not again!

Mason, with his hand still on my arm, yanked me up before I landed on the ground. For the third time my klutziness landed me in his arms, but this time I let myself enjoy his hard body pressed against me.

The fresh morning air must have done something to my head, because I felt woozy as he held me. My heart thumped and I forced myself to breathe normally. He didn't do or say anything. His eyes swept over my face as if he was trying to memorize it.

"I'll pick you up for dinner tomorrow night," he said.

He released his grip on me and reached out for the reins of his horse. Before I could say anything, he galloped out of the clearing.

I hated his cockiness and I couldn't stand how much I enjoyed being in his arms. But he filled me with a nervous excitement when I thought about dinner with him.

As I climbed back onto my horse and rode back to the ranch, I knew I needed to cancel. It wasn't just that he was a spoiled, rich jerk, with him getting the manager role that made him my boss. And if he was being honest about leaving, not only did I want to position myself to get his job, but I didn't want to get hurt. And just by the twinkle in his eyes, I knew he was someone who could break my heart without thinking twice about it.

Present Day

I expected Mason to be pushy and want to come into the cottage, but he only walked me to the door and left before I had time to ask if he wanted to come in for coffee.

The parallels between now and then were driving me crazy. I wanted to give in and go with it, to feel what it meant to be loved by him again, but I couldn't forget what it felt like to be left by him also.

The next day I asked Maya to take care of things for me while I figured out what I would wear on my date. Maya decided to stay after Ashley offered her a job and a room in the main house. I had to admit I missed having her in the cottage with me, even if it was cramped.

After spending the day shopping, I had a couple of new outfits picked out for the date. At the last minute, I decided to not make a big deal about it and just be comfortable. I put on my favorite pair of jeans and then looked in the mirror. My nose scrunched as I looked at my hair.

"Crap," I muttered as I pulled my hair out of the elastic. "What am I supposed to do with this?"

As I looked at my limp blonde hair in the mirror, the doorbell rang. Dammit, out of time! I flipped my head over and shook my fingers through my hair. Taking a quick glance at myself, I was surprised to find my hair looked a little better.

I opened the door and found Mason leaning against the frame. In his hand, he held three large sunflowers with dark purple irises. A thick yellow ribbon was tied around their stalks.

"Sunflowers?" I asked.

"I saw them and thought about that day in the field together. The day of the picnic. Remember?"

"How could I forget it? That was the first time we...well, you know."

"I can't believe you still can't say it," He laughed and gave me a sideways glance. "That was the first time we did it, had sex. Since you are a lady, I'll spare you the F word. It was the first time we made love."

"You can be such a girl sometimes," I said, taking the sunflowers and letting him into the cottage. "I'm surprised you even remember. I'm sure there were plenty of women after me."

"There's been no one since you. Every woman I've met has been compared to my memory of you. They didn't stand a chance."

"Are you telling me that for fifteen years you haven't, well, you know."

He laughed again. "What I'm telling you is that since being with you, I haven't made love with anyone else. Of course I've fucked--"

I put my hand up. "That's enough. I don't need to hear it."

"I am a man you know."

I brought the sunflowers into the kitchen and set them on the counter. I had one old vase that was collecting dust in the back of a cabinet. Cleaning the vase, I took the opportunity to glance over at Mason. His hands were in his pockets as he looked around my home.

I was surprised to see he wasn't in a suit, although I wasn't sure why I expected him to be. As I filled the vase with water, I realized what I said the other day was true. Despite how familiar he was to me, I didn't know much about this Mason. My memories were all about the man in his twenties, not the man almost in his forties.

"Where are we going for dinner?" I asked.

"On a picnic," he said.

He smiled and raised his eyebrows as his dimples deepened. My memories flooded me again, but I pushed them away. Tonight I was going to get to know Mason Abernathy again and leave the past behind.

Chapter Three

Mason

As I straightened my tie in the mirror, I heard the door to the suite open. It was Tricia. She knew I had my date with Tara tonight, and it was just like her to check up on me.

"You're wearing a suit?" she asked.

Her face was contorted in a way that told me much more than her four words had.

"It's what I always wear."

"Well, you're always working. You're not working tonight."

I sighed and took the tie off. "Tara never cared for the suits anyway."

In the months that Tricia had been working for me, we grew close. Growing up around so much wealth, I could easily spot those people who wanted to use me for it. Tricia was not one of them.

We talked a lot about our families and found many similarities between them. Tricia became the sister I never had and she finally had an older brother who could help her out. I found her family a nice home to live in in a suburb of Canyon Cove, and she never heard from their old landlord again. Once her father realized things had changed for the better, he became eager to get control over his habit and started attending Gamblers Anonymous meetings.

Her life had turned around and although she was working as my assistant, she also had plans to attend college. But she never let up on her promise to help me win Tara back. She called it her hobby. I didn't think I needed her help, but sometimes it was nice getting a woman's opinion on things.

"Where are you taking her?" she asked.

"That new place downtown."

"New place? That hoity toity French place? You're going to feed her snails? Mason, no woman in her right mind wants to eat snails."

"What about frog legs?" I asked, grinning.

"Now you're just being silly. You said you know her, what does she like to eat?"

"But this restaurant is beautiful, and I want to impress her."

"From what you've told me about her, that's not going to impress her at all. You want to impress her? Then show up with flowers."

"Flowers? Really? You don't think that's cliché?"

She shook her head at me. "I swear it's like you never dated in your life. I'll call The Dizzy Daisy while you change. They're on your way to Jefferson Manor."

"Pick something nice."

Tricia rolled her eyes at me and walked out of the bedroom. Other than a pair of jeans, all I had with me were suits. I pulled the jeans on and tucked in my buttoned shirt. As I put my boots on, Tricia called out to me.

"I gotta get home and make dinner. The flowers will be ready by the time you get there. I'm sure she'll love them. Now don't blow it."

As she was leaving, I crossed the room and grabbed the door handle to stop her. I opened my wallet and handed her a couple hundred dollar bills.

"Order something from the restaurant," I said. "I've taken up enough of your time with my personal stuff."

She hesitated for a moment as she looked at the cash.

"Just take it." I closed her fingers around the bills.

"Thank you," she whispered. "You know I'll--"

"I know, you keep telling me you'll pay me back. You don't have to, but if it makes you feel better saying it, that's fine. Now go."

As she left, I called down to the valet to have my car ready. I wanted everything to be perfect tonight with Tara. She had turned me down and canceled our date so many times since we met again, I didn't know if I'd get another chance with her.

I wasn't used to feeling like this. Normally I was confident and didn't care about anything but getting what I wanted. And I always got it. Tara was the first time I was afraid of losing something.

It was a short drive to the flower shop. A man wearing a dark green apron was bringing in the outside displays as I entered. With Halloween approaching, there were pumpkins of all sizes throughout the store.

"I'll be right with you," he said as he carried in a tall bucket of sunflowers.

"Can you make a bouquet from those?" I asked.

The sunflowers reminded me of a special day with Tara. One of the many I never forgot.

"Of course. I like pairing them with irises. I think the purple really makes them pop. By the way, are you Mr. Abernathy? Let me get the bouquet you ordered."

He disappeared into a back room and emerged with a large bouquet of yellow roses with red tips and silvery eucalyptus. It was beautiful, but the sunflowers had meaning to me.

"Do you deliver?" I asked.

"Sure, I do deliveries after we close."

I gave him Tricia's address and wrote out a card to her and slipped it in with the flowers.

Thanks, but I found something better.
Hope you enjoy them.
--Mason

As he rang me up, I looked around his shop and noticed a large wooden picnic basket.

"Is that for sale?" I asked.

"Whatever you see, you can buy. Except me of course," he said as he grabbed the basket and brought it over. "Planning a picnic?"

"Impromptu. Where I can get this filled for dinner?"

"My friend just opened a restaurant two doors down. His food is incredible." He handed me a menu. "You're going to need more than just the basket and food though. I'm sure I've got a blanket and some other things you can use."

By the time I left The Dizzy Daisy, my trunk was full of food, wine, and everything I could possibly need for my date with Tara.

***

"Where are we going for dinner?" she asked.

"On a picnic." I smiled and took her hand, happy to be near her again. "I've got everything in the car except for the most important part."

"If you say me, I swear I'll smack you."

I laughed. "I'll just shut up then."

As I opened the car door, I couldn't help but let my eyes wander over her. Her hair was loose and brushed her shoulders as she got into the car. She was curvier than I remembered, and I loved it. I wanted to grab her, hold her tight against me, and kiss her soft lips. But I knew from months ago that doing that could push her away. I would do anything to keep her here.

As I slowly drove over the long gravel driveway of Jefferson Manor to the main road, Tara settled into her seat. I wondered if she was as nervous as I was. Taking her out after so many years was like doing it for the first time again.

"Do you remember our first date?" I asked as I turned the car onto the twisting canyon road.

She was quiet for a moment and out of the corner of my eye, I could see her looking at me as if she thought I was up to something.

"Of course I do," she said. "We went to the steakhouse in town."

I chuckled. "No, I knew you'd get it wrong."

"There is no way I'm wrong. I remember that evening like it just happened yesterday."

"So do I, and that was not our first date. That had to be our third or fourth date." I turned quickly and our eyes met. She folded her arms in front of her and pretended to look annoyed. "I always loved how much we laughed together."

She laughed then elbowed me. "If I'm so wrong, why don't you tell me what our first date was."

"Well, since you needed to ask, I'll tell you. It was that morning that we rode the horses to the first clearing."

"Wait, are you talking about that first morning when we took the horses to the clearing and talked? I was just thinking about that the other day. That wasn't a date."

"It was to me. If it wasn't for that morning, you would've never agreed to go on another date with me."

She shook her head and laughed softly. "You're crazy."

"Maybe."

A few miles up the curving road, I turned at a large 'For Sale' sign and followed the dirt road further up a hill. The sun was beginning to set and while I knew it meant we had only a couple of hours, I wanted to bring Tara there.

I wanted to show her our future, even though I might not tell her about it just yet. Despite how much I wanted things between us to go back to the way they were, I could see Tara wanted to take things slow. I didn't blame her. She wasn't the only one who got hurt.

Chapter Four

Tara

Mason brought the car to a stop once we reached the top of the hill. Wildflowers and tall grass lined the dirt road.

"This is it," he said as he popped open the trunk.

"It reminds me of home," I said.

His hand covered mine on my lap and he smiled. "Me too."

He quickly turned away from me, and I knew there was something he wasn't saying. As he opened the car door, I caught the faint scent of the ocean.

"There's the big difference between here and home," he said as he looked in the distance.

The blue Pacific Ocean looked calm from the hilltop. I wasn't much of a swimmer or a beach person, but each time I saw the ocean it brought to me a calmness I couldn't explain.

Mason laid a blanket on the ground and began unloading his car. He had a large wooden basket with a hinged lid and a dark bottle of wine with an ivory label. None of the food mattered to me though, my stomach was flip flopping with nerves from being near him again.

"This is a big change from our first date," I said, sitting down on the thick wool blanket.

"Our first date?" he said with a smirk.

"Okay, our second date."

"I was going to take you to that new French place that opened up downtown, but I can see by how you're wrinkling your nose that I made the right choice."

I laughed. "You did. It's beautiful here. I never cared for all that fancy stuff anyway."

Using a battery-powered corkscrew, Mason opened the bottle of wine, then poured the dark red liquid into two glasses. He handed me a glass with a mischievous grin.

"Thank you," I said as I took the glass.

I looked at the wine and could smell a strong aroma of cherries and roses. I never cared much for wine, especially the red variety, which tasted too heavy to me. As I carefully balanced the glass on the ground beside me, Mason let out a loud laugh.

"You really haven't changed at all," he said.

"What are you talking about? I have changed. I am a completely different person than the Tara you knew long ago."

"You still hate wine, don't you?"

I closed my eyes briefly as I nodded, realizing his point. "Just because I still don't like wine doesn't mean the rest of me hasn't changed."

He reached for one of the grocery bags and pulled out a six-pack of Pepsi.

"I got this for you. It's still cold," he said before reaching into the bag again and pulling out a bag of flexible straws. "And I got these for you too." He opened a can of soda and handed it to me along with the bag of straws.

I dropped a straw into the can and took a sip as I looked at Mason. The lines around his eyes were more visible now that the sun cast shadows as it set. Despite his looking older, he was still the best-looking man I had ever seen. It didn't matter how much time had passed, I still felt like that girl meeting him for the first time. Without thinking, I put my hand on my chest to try to calm my pounding heart.

"I knew I did good," he said.

"You haven't changed at all. You're as cocky as ever," I said. He raised a questioning eyebrow at me and I lowered my hand from my heart. "Don't get all excited, it's just the caffeine."

"If you say so." He opened another can of soda and took a long drink. "I've been thinking a lot about you lately. About us, to be honest."

I put my hand up. "Just stop right there. You know I want to take things slow."

"I know, I know. It's taken you months just to say yes to a date. I think I understand what you mean by slow."

I felt a little guilty for making him wait for so long. Looking at him now, I couldn't remember why I found it so hard to keep the hurt I felt in the past where it belonged.

"Since you seem to remember so much about our dates, why don't you tell me which one was your favorite?" I asked.

He looked thoughtfully for a minute before his mouth spread into a big grin. His brown eyes caught the sun and twinkled, reminding me of the beach long ago. I looked out towards the ocean as he spoke.

"I don't have to tell you. I know it's your favorite date too."

"That was more than a date, you took me to another country. And you tricked me into going."

"As you know, I'll do whatever I have to to get what I want. Back then, what I wanted was you."

"And now?"

"I shouldn't have to answer that." His voice was serious. "I've never wanted anything but you. Now or then it doesn't make a difference. But whatever happens between us, I'll never forget the time we shared together. And I'll always hold close to me the time we spent at Mallorca."

Fifteen Years Ago

Mason stormed into the tack room where I was finishing up my day. It had been a couple of weeks since we started working together and things had changed since that first ride we took together, but not for the better. After I canceled our date, he went from hot to cold without any notice.

While I enjoyed having him around as eye candy, there were times where I was reminded that he was my boss. I didn't like those times and by the fierce look in his eye I knew this was going to be one of them.

"I'm going to need you to work overtime this week starting tomorrow," he said.

"I have the day off tomorrow. I'm taking my father to his check-up."

I didn't look at Mason as I wiped down the saddle I used earlier. It was easier to say no to him when I wasn't staring at his gorgeous face.

"Reschedule it," he said. "There's a horse I want, and we have to leave tomorrow to get it or they'll sell it to someone else."

"No, I have to take him. No horse is that important. You have people knocking your doors down for the breeds you have here. You don't need more."

"I know what I need," he growled.

His voice gave me goose bumps. I stopped what I was doing and before I realized it, I had turned around to face him. He was standing so close to me I could swear I felt the heat of his body through my clothes, but maybe that was just wishful thinking.

He was in a dark brown suit that made him look both dressed up and casual at the same time. His jacket was open and his white shirt unbuttoned low enough that I found myself staring at his collarbone and wishing I could see more.

"What do you need?" I asked, my voice hoarse.

I cleared my throat and mentally kicked myself for sounding like a moron. As hard as I tried to make my voice sound normal when Mason was around, it didn't.

No matter what we talked about, there was always a point in our conversation where his voice would change. I couldn't explain it, but something in his timbre would turn me into a blathering idiot. I was always fine until he did that, after which I was done. He always had that effect on me and although he never pointed it out, I knew he could tell.

"I need you to pack for three days away. Do you have a passport? We're heading to Spain," he said.

"Spain? For a horse?"

"I heard a breeder there has a Menorquín horse. They are extremely rare, almost extinct. No more questions about this, it's part of your job to help me acquire new horses. My limo will pick you up in the morning."

Morning? Suddenly my brain switched back on.

"I can't go. My parents need me."

"They'll be fine without you. It's only a few days."

He walked out of the tack room before I could argue more. I didn't know what to do. How could I leave for another country in the morning? I needed more time to make sure my family would be alright without me.

***

As I rushed into the house, the screen door slammed shut behind me.

"Sorry," I yelled, worried my father might have been napping.

"We're in the kitchen," my mother called out.

As I walked in, I was surprised to see my sister and my niece Maya. Brooke had my same blonde hair, but her eyes were wider apart than mine. She had left home at eighteen when I was just a little younger than Maya. Unfortunately our age difference kept us from being close growing up.

Maya was ten years old and very shy. Her dark blonde hair was pulled into pigtails that hung in long, springy curls.

"I didn't know you were coming, Brooke," I said.

"Call it spur of the moment," she said with a smile. "I'm almost done making dinner too so you're just in time." Her eyes darted to the table where our parents were talking to Maya. "Can we talk privately?"

"Sure, let's go out on the porch," I said.

Brooke lowered the flame on the stove and then joined me on the screened-in porch. The crisp night air gave me a chill, and I rubbed my arms to warm myself.

"I know I haven't been around much since Craig and I got married," she said. "I'm really sorry about that. I know it's been rough on you having to take care of them."

"I never blamed you or anything like that. You were eighteen when you moved out. I was younger than Maya at that time, so this is just how it's always been. You have no reason to feel sorry."

"I know it's been rough though. I got to move out and live my life while you were stuck here."

"I never thought I was stuck. I have a job that I love and I got it because of them. If they hadn't bought me Ladyfinger, I would've never started working at Abernathy Ranch. What's this all about anyway, Brooke? What's going on?"

She sighed and turned to look back in the house before speaking.

"I'm leaving Craig," she said. "I haven't told them yet."

Brooke hesitated like she was going to say something else then changed her mind. Her eyes darted across the yard then to the street before they came back to me.

"You're leaving a lot out, aren't you?"

"You were probably too young to remember," she said. "Mom and Dad didn't want me marrying Craig. They said we were too young, we had our whole lives ahead of us, they just went on and on. If I tell them that we're divorcing, they're going to give me even more grief."

"Give them a break, you've been married for over ten years now. I don't think they'll give you shit about leaving him. If you feel it's what you need to do, then that's good enough."

She nodded her head then pushed her long hair back behind her ear. As she did that, I saw a bruise at her hairline by her neck.

"Wait," I said as I reached out to her. "How'd you get that? Did he hit you?"

Her hand went to her neck and she pulled her hair forward so it fell around her shoulders. I could tell she was thinking over what she was going to say next as her eyes darted to the street again. I gave her the stern look I learned from our dad.

"Oh wow, that's exactly the look I was trying to avoid," she said.

"Has he hit Maya?" I asked.

"No, no, I don't think he would ever do that."

"You don't think? That's not something you're sure of?"

"Listen, Tara, you don't understand. I love him. He's my first love, my first everything. But when he drinks, he's a different person. It's like I don't even know him. He doesn't mean to do it, he just can't control himself."

"That's bullshit, Brooke. If he has a drinking problem, he should get help. But if he's hitting you, then you need to fucking leave. Pardon my French. How'd you get this?"

I pushed her hair back and tilted her head to get a better look. The bruise was already turning yellow. It wasn't fresh.

"That was a beer bottle. It was my fault, I forgot to buy more beer when I did the grocery shopping," she said.

"Brooke! I'm so mad at you right now." I squeezed her tight as I hugged her. "You're an idiot, okay? You and Maya can stay in my room with me. Your old bed is still in there."

She shivered as I held her and then soft sobs came from her throat.

"I was hoping we could stay here. I know there's not much room, but we don't have anywhere to go," she said.

"You can stay here as long as you like. This is your home too, you know."

"Thanks, sis." She breathed in deep and wiped the tears from her face. "He doesn't know we left. He'd been gone for two days and I know what that means. I didn't want to be there when he came home. And then there's Maya. I have to do what's right for her. I don't want her thinking this is normal."

"You did the right thing by leaving. Let's get back in, it's chilly out here."

As I reached for the door to head back into the house, she grabbed my hand.

"Wait. I just need a few more minutes to compose myself. I don't want Maya to see that I was crying. She's very sensitive. Why don't you tell me what's going on with you. Are you dating anyone?"

Mason popped into my head, and I smiled even though I didn't mean to.

"Ahhh, I know that look," Brooke said. "Who is he?"

"No one. I'm not dating anyone." No matter how hard I tried, I couldn't stop smiling.

"Then who are you thinking about? You're crushing on someone. I can tell."

"I was just thinking about the new manager at work."

"At the ranch?"

I nodded and despite how much I fought it, I grinned.

"I wanted to hate him for being a cocky, spoiled bastard, but there's just something about him. He's smart and funny and he's just a couple of years older than me. And oh my lord, is he hot. He looks at me and I just melt into a puddle."

She giggled. "This is exactly what I needed to hear. What's his name? And when do I get to meet him?"

"Mason Abernathy. And why would you meet him? He's just my boss. Although he's coming in the morning to pick me up, but now that you're here, I think I'm going to push back on him more about going. I didn't want to leave Mom and Dad anyway."

"Abernathy? Really?" Her eyebrows shot up in surprise. "Where is this wealthy rancher taking my little sister?"

"Oh stop," I said. "He's looking to buy a horse. He said we have to go to Spain for it."

"Spain? To buy a horse? Well, that's the biggest load of horse shit I've ever heard, Tara."

"I didn't make that up."

"I didn't say you did, but I know guys. He's not looking for a horse, he's looking to spend some time with you. He's whisking you off somewhere romantic. I know it!"

"You're insane. There's plenty of romantic places right here in North Carolina. Why would he take me all the way to Europe?"

"Because he's a billionaire," she said as she shrugged. "They do things we normal people would never understand. Now let's go eat and then get you packed. There's no way you're not going and now that I'm here, you won't have to worry about Mom and Dad."

***

I couldn't sleep, so I stared at the ceiling as I listened to Brooke and Maya's steady breathing in the next bed. I was glad they were sound asleep. They needed the rest. I couldn't imagine what they had been through with Craig, but I hoped it was over. Even with my father as ill as he was, I knew he would do anything to protect them. They were safe.

As the sun began seeping through the blinds, Brooke stretched and quietly rolled out of bed. She peeked out the window and started flapping her hands excitedly.

"What is it?" I whispered.

Maya groaned and rolled over. Brooke tiptoed out of the room and waved at me to follow. She closed the door as quietly as she could, then yanked me by the arm to a window in the kitchen.

"Look outside," she said.

I braced myself. I expected to see Craig out there in his beat up Ford, but instead I saw a long limousine with its glossy paint shining in the rising sun.

"That must've made a wrong turn somewhere," I said.

"That's for you, Tara." She smacked the back of my head.

"Hey, that wasn't nice."

"Sometimes we all need a good smack to the head. You said Mason Abernathy was picking you up this morning, and it's morning."

"But it's a limo."

"What did you think he was going to show up in? A Chevy pick-up?"

"I didn't really think about it," I said, feeling foolish. "If it is him, he's early."

I slipped on a sweater and went out into the cool morning air. As I got closer to the limo, a window at the back rolled down, revealing Mason.

"I know I'm early. I couldn't sleep," he said. "How quickly can you get ready?"

"I couldn't sleep either. I'm mostly packed, I just need to shower. Give me twenty minutes?"

He nodded, and the window rose as I turned back to the house. As I entered, Brooke was waiting for me.

"Wow, you weren't kidding about him," she said, fanning herself. "What did he say?"

"He couldn't sleep. I have to go get ready."

"Oh, he's totally into you." She followed me through the house as I collected my things for the trip.

"I think being gone from home has made you crazy. He didn't say that at all."

"He said he couldn't sleep and you said he wants you to get ready quickly. He was thinking about you all night long."

"I have to shower," I said. "He can have his pick of any of the beautiful socialites in and probably outside of North Carolina. There is no way he was thinking about me last night."

"I'm telling you, you're wrong. I know guys."

As Brooke made kissing sounds, I pushed her out of the bathroom and locked the door. The last thing I needed was her filling my head with ridiculous ideas about Mason. It was bad enough I was attracted to him.

***

The limo ride, the private jet, everything overwhelmed me so much that it was a blur. When we arrived at the airport in Spain, I realized I knew nothing about the trip or this horse we were looking to buy.

"What kind of horse are we here for?" I asked.

"It's a Menorquín. We'll be heading to Menorca for it."

"A Menorquín? I've never heard of that breed."

"They're rare and in danger of extinction. That's why we're here. There are very few Menorquín horses left and the majority of them are still only on the island, but I plan to look on the other islands as well."

"Islands?"

"Yes, Mallorca, Ibiza, I'm sure you've heard of them. We'll be taking a boat," he said.

Mason pointed out the window. In the distance, white boats dotted the blue-green sea. The view looked like a living postcard.

The more I looked, the more out of place I felt. Those boats didn't look anything like what my father and I had gone fishing in. And as the limo parked at the dock, all I saw were fancy people in their beautiful clothing. I felt uncomfortable. I was wearing my favorite pair of jeans and a plaid shirt that had been washed so many times it had gone soft. I didn't fit in.

"I don't think I packed appropriately," I said, thinking about my clothes that were perfect for the ranch and not much else.

"You have nothing to worry about," he said. "It's just going to be you and me. We'll be staying here overnight and then in the morning, the yacht will arrive."

Yacht?

Money never intimidated me. I knew the Abernathys were just like everyone else, they put their pants on one leg at a time. But hearing Mason talk about taking a yacht like it was something normal was the final push after a long and overwhelming day.

"I think maybe I should go home," I said. "I really don't belong here."

"I don't want to hear that. If you're worried about your parents, you can call home once we get to the hotel room."

"Hotel room? Not rooms? Don't you think that's a little presumptuous of you to think I would share a room with you? You told me we were here for work."

The car stopped in front of a tall building. Without answering me, Mason got out of the car, and a bellhop headed straight for our bags. He entered the hotel lobby and I followed behind him, waiting for him to respond. Had we been anywhere else, I would have made a scene. Mason was lucky I felt out of my element.

We rode up the elevator in silence. Each bell that indicated we were passing another floor made my anger build even more. Who did he think he was? Was he that cocky that he thought women were ready to sleep with him at the drop of a hat? I didn't care how gorgeous he was, he would have to earn it.

The elevator door opened. At the end of the richly carpeted hall, the bellhop was opening a hotel room door. Despite how many times I glared at Mason, he kept ignoring me. He walked ahead and entered the room while I was still making my way down the hall.

Before I reached the door, the attendant exited into the hall with his cart and tipped his hat at me. I entered the room ready to blow up.

I expected a typical hotel room with a bed or two and a desk crammed in the corner. I didn't expect to see a room that was larger than my parent's entire house.

The luggage were stacked in a corner by the bar. At the far end of the room was a wall of windows that looked out to the marina below. Mason stood in front of the window watching the ships as they docked.

"The bedrooms are on either side of this room. You can pick whichever one you want," he said.

The main room had stunned me so much that I didn't realize there weren't any beds. At each turn I felt more out of my element.

I entered one of the bedrooms and immediately knew that was the one. I didn't care if the other one was larger, better, or anything. As soon as I saw the plush king-sized bed with an array of soft pillows on it, I jumped on the bed and curled up with them.

"Don't fall asleep," Mason said from the doorway.

"I won't," I said, stifling a yawn.

"I made reservations for us for dinner. But maybe I should cancel them."

"Reservations?" After everything I had seen that day, I had an idea of what to expect at a restaurant. "I didn't bring anything nice to wear. You said we were here to look at a horse."

His brows knitted as he rubbed his chin.

"Then we'll have dinner here. Just the two of us," he said.

Something in the way he looked at me told me he wasn't telling me everything. He turned to walk out of the room as I sat up in bed.

"Wait," I said.

When he didn't listen, I threw a pillow at him and it smacked him in the back of his head. He bent down to pick up the pillow and walked it back to me.

"Yes?" he said, looking amused.

"You're lying about the horse, aren't you?"

"You turned me down for dinner," he said. "But I always get what I want."

"What about the horse?"

"He's not invited."

"You know what I mean."

"There is no horse. What I told you about the Menorquín horse is true, but I was just looking for an excuse to take you away."

"You could have made that excuse somewhere local, you know."

"I liked the idea of having you trapped here, far from home."

He grinned evilly as he turned and walked towards the door. I flung another pillow at his head but missed.

We spent the night talking and to my surprise, we had a lot in common. Mason was very down to earth. After we ate, he got up and walked to the window and peered out at the twinkling lights below.

"Did you bring a jacket?" he asked. "It's chilly out, but I've always loved the beach at night. Let's go for a walk."

Since I didn't bring anything, Mason let me borrow a sweatshirt he brought with him. We went down the elevator and walked along the docks until we reached the beach.

The white sand glowed in the moonlight. I shivered from the cold and Mason put his arm around my shoulders.

"Why aren't you like this at home?" I asked.

"Like what?"

"Like a normal person. You're such a jerk at the ranch, I'm never sure what to expect from you."

He nodded slowly but didn't speak. I waited for him to say something, but the more time that passed, the more annoyed I got.

"Aren't you going to say something?" I asked.

He shrugged. "I don't have anything to say. You're right."

"I'm right? You are a jerk?"

"It's not the first time I've heard it."

"And?"

"And it's how I am," he said.

He leaned forward and our eyes met. Behind his piercing gaze, I saw sadness. With a sigh, he pushed his hands into his jeans pockets then tilted his head to look at me out of the corner of his eye.

"Tara, you already know I haven't been home for many years. You've met my mother, so I'm sure it's not a surprise that she's the reason." He sighed again and ran his fingers through his hair. "I've never told this to anyone, but I haven't been back home in six years because I needed to get away from her. She is a pathetic, mean person, and nothing matters to her more than herself."

"I'm sorry," I said, wishing I had something better to say.

"She's controlled my father for as long as I can remember, and she tried to control me too. The only time she ever wanted me around when I was a kid was when it made a picture perfect moment. I know it's ridiculous. I realize I am a grown man now, but somehow her words still cut me and turn me into that little boy all over again. And that's the last thing I want. I can't explain it, but no matter how much I know who and how she is, I'm always hoping she will change. I always want to give her the benefit of the doubt."

He shook his head and mumbled something I couldn't hear.

"I don't know why I'm telling you all of this. We hardly know each other, but I want to change that. That's what this trip is all about. I can't stop thinking about you, and sometimes that pisses me off. So I don't mean anything by it, but that's why sometimes I'm a prick."

"You're a prick because thinking about me makes you mad? That's really not something someone wants to hear when they've been flown thousands of miles from home," I said, trying to make him laugh.

He stopped walking and turned to stand in front of me. There was no humor in his expression.

"It pisses me off because your life is at the ranch and that's the last place I want to be," he said. "I'm torn between leaving the ranch or staying to spend time with you."

We didn't talk for the rest of our walk on the beach. A gust of wind swept across the water, and I wrapped my arms around myself. Mason slipped his arms back around me again.

"Let's go back to the room," he whispered.

When we got back to the hotel, the woman at the front desk waved us over. She had a slip of paper in her hand.

"I have a message for you, Mr. Abernathy," she said.

"I told you to not disturb me until morning," Mason growled.

"She said it was an emergency."

The clerk handed the note to Mason, and he shoved it into his back pocket without reading it.

As we rode the elevator up to our room, he pressed me against the wall and his lips closed over mine softly. But I couldn't stop thinking about the note.

"You have to read it," I said.

"No, no good can come of it. Not at this hour."

"But she said it was an emergency."

"She said she, and that means it was my mother. Everything with her is an emergency."

"Still, I think you should read it to make sure."

As we entered the room, he pulled the note out of his back pocket. He unfolded it and as he read it, the color drained from his face.

"What is it?" I asked.

"It's my father. We have to fly back now. He's in the hospital and my mother said it doesn't look good."

Mason called a private airline and arranged for a plane to fly us back to the States that night. He retreated into himself and didn't speak, but he held my hand during the entire flight.

It was late when we got to the hospital. Even though it was past visiting hours, Mason walked through the lobby towards the elevators. No one stopped him. He seemed to know exactly where he was heading.

As the doors opened to the floor, I saw a placard with his last name on it. It was easy for me to forget that the Abernathy family owned everything in town.

"Which room?" Mason asked a nurse as we walked past the nurses' station.

Her face had a momentary look of confusion until he recognized him.

"Oh, I'm sorry, Mr. Abernathy," she said. "Your father is in 402."

We hurried down the hall. Once we were in front of the room, Mason took a deep breath, composing himself, before entering.

"Mason?" his dad said, looking up from a crossword puzzle. "What are you doing here? I thought you were away. Oh hello, Tara, I didn't see you there."

"I heard you weren't well. What's going on?" Mason asked.

"I'm as well as can be expected, son. I had a kidney stone so they admitted me, but it's nothing serious. You didn't have to come home."

"Mother said..." Mason's voice trailed off and he gritted his teeth. "Where is she?"

"You know your mother hates hospitals. I'm sure she's at home."

Mason stormed out of the room, and I raced after him. I finally caught up to him at the elevators.

"This is exactly what I was talking about," he said as he paced. "I'm sorry about this. This didn't turn out how I wanted at all, but I swear I'll make it up to you."

Present Day

The sun cast sparkles in the ocean as it slowly descended. I stood and brushed myself off as I took a final look around. The hill was getting darker and shadowy. In the distance, the lights from the city twinkled. Dusk had always been my favorite time of day and on top of this hill with the ocean and city lights, it felt magical.

I thought about how much I kept trying to tell Mason that I was different. I kept trying to convince him I wasn't the girl I was all those years ago. But what I didn't think about was how much I loved that arrogant young man in the past. Despite my pushing him to see who I was now, I never thought about how he had changed, too. While he was still as confident and cocky as ever, for the first time I realized how much I really meant to him.

Mason packed the car back up and then we were on our way down the dirt road. When he stopped at the canyon road, I noticed the large 'For Sale' sign and wondered how I had missed it earlier.

"Jeez, that hill is for sale?" I muttered.

"That's how I found out about that view," he said. "I've been looking for land in Canyon Cove. I'm thinking about building here."

"Building? You mean a ranch?"

"Yes, Abernathy West. I'll build an eco-friendly ranch and move the horses here." He reached over and placed his hand over mine before intertwining our fingers together. "I've been thinking about the future, and it's right here in Canyon Cove with you."

Chapter Five

Tara

The future with me?

The man I had been dreaming about for the past fifteen years just said the words I had wanted to hear years ago, but now I wasn't so sure. A future with Mason was exactly what I always wanted. But with him talking about building a ranch and including me in his plans, I felt like he was making my decisions for me. I couldn't help but revolt.

"Wait," I said as I tried to clear my head. "What do you mean with me?"

He glanced at me, then back at the road. I recognized worry in his eyes and wished I could take the words back. Buying a damn hill and building a ranch had to take time, what was I so worried about?

"Tara, I'm not going to make it a big secret that I want a future with you. I understand you need things to move at your own pace and I'm willing to wait until you say you're ready, but that doesn't mean I'm going to stop my plans."

"What about my plans? Did you ever think of asking me what my plans for the future are?"

"I'm sorry, I didn't think my moving to Canyon Cove would change anything for you. Except hopefully your home address."

"I...it..." I stammered as I worked out what to say. I just wanted to argue with him, but I wasn't making sense even to myself. Eventually I went with an old argument I knew I could win. "You never think about how things affect anyone else. You always just figure you can throw some money at the problem and it'll be taken care of."

"What are you talking about?"

"You and your money. You think you can just move out here and dictate whatever you want."

"I'm not dictating anything. I'm building a home, and I would like you to be a part of that. If you don't want to, then I'll just be glad to be near you."

"Don't give me that crap. You have no idea what it's like. You've always had an easy life."

"I'm not going to apologize for my wealth. Where is all this coming from?"

"From you wanting me to move in. I know it's not that easy or simple. I will never fit into your world."

"Fit into my world? We're from the same world."

"No, we're not. We're from two entirely different worlds. I worked my ass off to help support my parents and you got to travel the world and do whatever you want. You never had anything to worry about. You could never understand."

"Don't tell me this is about money. There's something you're not telling me."

"I can't tell you," I said. "Just trust me, I don't fit in. I never fit in."

"What makes you think that? I never did anything to make you feel that way, did I?"

"No, you never did, but...never mind."

"What is it? Did someone tell you that? Tell me who and I'll hand their ass over to them."

"No one. Forget I said anything. Just take me home, please."

"Tara…" he pleaded.

Just the way he spoke my name, his voice said so many things to me. He squeezed my hand, but he didn't say anything else. I couldn't tell him the truth of what happened all those years ago. I couldn't admit that if it wasn't for his mother, things might have been different. I had kept that secret for so many years there was no reason to reveal it now.

Fifteen Years Ago

"Damn mud," I grumbled.

I was cleaning out the shoe of one of our new horses when I heard the loud thud of Mason's boots on the barn's wood floor. As I raked the brush at an angle under the horse's hoof, Mason stopped at the stall door.

"Tara, finish up there and come to my office," he said. "It's important."

Once I was done with the horse, I cleaned up and went to find Mason. Just as I stepped foot inside his office, he grabbed my arm, pulled me close, and kissed me.

"Stop that," I said. "We're at work."

"That just makes me want to do more." He laughed and pressed his lips against mine. "Pack your bag for the weekend."

"For the weekend? You know I have to take care of my parents."

"Don't worry about them. I already talked to Lucy, and she said she'd stay with them again."

"You really take care of everything, don't you?"

Even though I meant it as a joke, I couldn't help but be bothered a little by it. I was used to taking care of my parents and myself. I didn't like someone else making decisions for me.

"I do," he said with a grin. "We're going to the Kentucky Derby. It's a family tradition, we do it every May."

"The Derby?" I stepped back and shook my head. "I can't go. I can't be there with you and your family. I don't even think your mother likes me."

"She doesn't have to like you. I want you there. Even my father thought it was a great idea. He thinks you'll love it."

How could I tell him that the Derby was more than just a Thoroughbred race, it was one of the most talked-about fashion events in the South? I looked down at my scuffed boots while I tried to think of a way out. Mason lifted my chin and I looked up into his gentle brown eyes. He looked concerned.

"Are you worried you won't find a large enough hat?" he asked. "Because my mother said you could borrow something of hers."

I wrinkled my nose and frowned. While I would love to go to the Derby, the thought of wearing something of his mother's made me cringe.

"I'll have to think about it," I said. "When are you leaving?"

"Tomorrow." He opened the closet door and pulled out a long bag on a hanger. "I got this for you." He lifted the bag and revealed a sleeveless blue dress. "Can you imagine what a nightmare it would be for me if you wore something of my mother's and I thought you looked hot in it? I'd probably end up in therapy for years."

"I can't believe you did this," I said as I touched the dress's soft fabric.

"I invited you to go to the Derby at the last minute, so I had to make sure you had something to wear. I ordered a hat from a local salon, but that will be delivered to the hotel. Do you need anything else?"

I shook my head, too stunned to answer.

"Good," he said. "Then like I said earlier, pack your bag for the weekend."

***

The trip flew by and the next thing I knew, I was getting ready to watch the Kentucky Derby. Never in a million years did I ever think I would set foot in Churchill Downs.

The dress fit me perfectly. I wore my hair swept over my shoulder. Just before the limo arrived, I placed the large brimmed ivory-colored hat with an oversized blue ribbon bow on my head. I felt a little ridiculous with the size of the hat, but I had to admit it was fun to wear.

As I carefully slid into the limo, I ended up with Mason's mother Iris on one side of me and Mason on the other. I smiled warmly at her, but she turned away as if I wasn't there. Once the car started on its way, she reached into her clutch and pulled out a small hand mirror.

"I'm glad you could make it this year, Mason," she said.

"I know it bothers you that I've been away so long."

"The least you could do was come visit. And what about poor Chloe?"

"What about her? You know I came home to help her with her brother. Once everything's set with him, I plan on leaving again."

"Oh yes, Rif Raf."

"Rafa."

"Whatever," she said as she dabbed at her lipstick. "Well, the least you could have done was bring Chloe. She always loved the Derby."

Mason didn't reply, and I was left sitting between them wondering if I had developed a super power of invisibility. I thought Chloe was just a friend of Mason's, but the way his mother spoke about her, I wondered if she was more.

Even as my head spun with my questions about Chloe, I couldn't help but wonder what my expiration date with Mason was. I knew he had plans to go to Germany, but in the two months we had been together, we had never discussed his leaving.

As the limo approached Churchill Downs' front entrance gate, Mason's father leaned over to look out the window.

"Mason, before I lose you for the rest of the day to your lovely date, I'd like to introduce you to some friends of mine."

Mason turned to look at me and I nodded, letting him know I was fine.

"Don't worry about her, dear," Iris said. "I'll keep her company."

I forced a smile at Mason, hoping he would be reassured. He squeezed my hand then leaned closer to me, dipping his head underneath my hat.

"I promise I'll only be a few minutes," he whispered.

I got out of the car and watched as Mason's father introduced him to several men. Just beyond them I saw their wives talking together like they were all old friends. Each of them was dressed to impress.

"You know, you should have told my son you couldn't come," Iris said.

"Why would I do that?"

"Because you don't belong here. I'm glad Mason has found slumming it to be a nice enough distraction that he's still at home, but don't forget where you come from."

My first instinct was to say nothing and just take however she treated me. But the devil on my shoulder smacked that instinct away and told me to stand up for myself.

"Excuse me?" I said.

I met her gaze straight on, daring her to turn away from me.

"I'll just remind you that my son needed to dress you up like a Barbie for you to even attend. Or maybe that's why you're here. You found a way to get your raise after all."

She turned and walked away, but I stormed after her.

"How dare you talk to me that way. Don't you walk away from me," I said.

Iris joined the women I had been looking at earlier, and they greeted her with air kisses. I stopped myself and glared at her. She was right, I didn't belong there.

"There you are," Mason said as he slipped his arm around my waist. "Everything alright?"

I looked up at him, then back to his mother with her friends. She could think I was only interested in her son for his money all she wanted. I knew it wasn't true, but what she said cut me deep. She hit all of my insecurities and her words echoed in my head.

"Everything's fine," I said, forcing a smile again.

"Let's go look at the horses. I'm thinking about buying a couple."

"From the race? No one is going to sell a winning horse."

"I'm not looking for the winners, I like the losers."

"Why would you want a loser?"

He pulled me closer to him as we walked.

"You know all of this is my father's and it was his father's before him. I love horses, they're in my blood. But I don't like how people treat them once that horse loses value to its owner. I know you know what I'm talking about. The life of a racehorse, for example, is a great one. Those horses live to race, it's in their blood no different than raising horses is in mine. But that doesn't mean they should be slaughtered just because they don't earn money."

"Of course I agree with you. You know I give just as much care to our pasture puffs as I do our Thoroughbreds. I'm always surprised at how many older horses we have on the ranch."

"We should have more," he said. "Abernathy Ranch will be mine one day and when it is, you'll see how things will change. There's no reason these horses should have nowhere to go once they're retired."

I admired him. Not many ranchers would think like that. Those old horses affect the bottom line, and I was glad to see that Mason cared more about the animals than his bank account.

As we walked along the backside, I felt more at home. The elegance and wealth that the Derby was known for wasn't back here. All there was were the horses, their riders, and their owners. It reminded me of the ranch back home and Iris's words echoed in my head again.

"When are you leaving?" I asked.

Mason stopped. He frowned as he gently touched my chin.

"Did my mother say something?"

I couldn't answer him. Despite everything, Iris was his mother and I couldn't tell him the things she said to me. I wasn't even sure if he would believe me.

"No, but you did say once Rafa was settled, you were going."

"I did say that, but to tell you the truth, he's been settled for some time. I've done what I can and his sister can take care of anything else with him. I haven't left yet because I don't want to. The past two months with you have meant more to me than anything. I was supposed to head to Germany in May, but I postponed it. The next start is October, but I don't know. I don't want to be so far from you."

"That first day we spoke, you said it was what you really wanted. You have to do it."

"When the time is right, I'll go. Right now what I really want is right here in front of me."

Present Day

Mason drove in silence towards Jefferson Manor. When he pulled up in front of the cottage, he moved the shifter into park but didn't say a word. I knew he was leaving everything up to me. After my blow up, I couldn't blame him. I felt bad about letting my emotions get the best of me.

"Why don't you come in? We still need to catch up," I said.

Once we were inside, I busied myself with readying a pot of tea. I had ordered some pastries from Mirabella's just in case I invited Mason in, so I set them out on a plate. The cottage was small, but it was open, with no walls separating the great room and the kitchen. While I got everything ready, Mason looked at my family photos on the fireplace.

"Are your parents still alive?" he asked as he held up a photo. "When was this taken?"

From across the room I recognized a photo from Medieval Times, the family dinner and show theater.

"That was five years ago, just before I started working here. I did a lot of different jobs after I left Abernathy." I set the small round table and we sat down across from each other. "My father passed away a month after that picture was taken."

"What about your mom?"

"She's good. Something happened when he died and she changed. I think she realized how short life really is and thought she was missing out on a lot. She travels all the time now. I never know where she is until she calls, and she never stays anywhere for very long.

"What about your parents? I've heard that after all these years of dying, your father is still alive."

Mason laughed as he nodded. "He is and surprisingly well. He's very frail, but since my mother left him, he's a new man. They both still live at Abernathy Ranch, but they live separate lives."

"What about you? Did you ever marry? Are you living at the ranch too?"

"No," he said.

I waited for him to continue. Instead he squeezed lemon into his tea and took a sip.

"No? No what?"

"No to everything. I never married. I never lived at the ranch."

I stared at him blankly as I tried to make sense of his words. I wanted to know what happened to him since I last saw him, but he wasn't telling me enough. I needed details and I hated to ask for them, but he wasn't giving me much choice.

"Then what did you do for all these years?"

"I've traveled a lot. I never went back to North Carolina. I stayed on the road and moved from hotel to hotel, staying wherever I needed to do business. I put everything into my work and never married."

"I never got married either."

"You didn't?" He looked away and then his face hardened. He clenched and unclenched his jaw before standing. "I'm sorry, I have to go."

"What do you mean? What just happened? Did I say something wrong?"

"I have to get going. Thank you for joining me for dinner."

As I stood from the table, Mason crossed the room and walked out the door. I raced to the door, but by the time I opened it, I saw his taillights moving up the long driveway towards the road.

I didn't know what happened. I thought again about what I said and was left with only my confusion.

"If only I could read minds," I said.

Closing the door, I heard my cell phone chime.

Mason: I'm sorry. I owe you an explanation, but right now I'm the one who needs a little time.

I stared at the message for a while but didn't know how to respond. It was an emotional day. Maybe we both needed a break.

Chapter Six

Mason

She never got married?

I spent all these years without her, not even looking for her because I thought she was happily married. Had I known she wasn't, I would have moved mountains to find her.

Arriving at the hotel, I looked towards the bar and thought about having a drink to cool off. Instead I pushed that thought out of my mind. I wanted to be angry at the time we lost. Most of all, I wanted to be furious with myself for not looking for the one woman I had always loved.

Fifteen Years Ago

"I am not staying. I'll be here for a couple of months and then I'm going to Germany," I said. "Deutschland Industrial is doing some very advanced environmental things. They have very set guidelines for when investors can visit, and I don't want to lose out on this opportunity."

My mother's face dropped and for a moment I thought she was going to cry. It was the usual emotional blackmail I had dealt with my entire life and the reason I hadn't been home in six years.

On the other hand, my father stared at me blankly from behind his desk. The enormity of it made him appear that much smaller and frail. It was a look he used to his advantage far too often.

"Then you'll have a couple of months working here," he said.

"You realize I have my own company now. I don't have the time to do your grunt work as some sort of proving ground for a job I don't want."

"It doesn't matter if you don't want it, one day all of Abernathy Ranch will be yours. You need to learn everything about it just like I did and--"

"And your father did before you. I know, Dad, I've heard this all before."

"Mason, I don't think you understand. A lot is at stake with the ranch, and I won't be around forever. I don't have much time left."

I sat down and pressed the heels of my hands into my eyes. I loved my parents, I really did, but they drove me crazy. The longer I had been away from home, the more eccentric they became.

"Did Doctor Elias say that?" I asked.

"No, but anything can happen. I am not a young man."

For as long as I could remember, my father was dying. It was how he guilted me into doing things for the ranch and learning how it operated. There wasn't a job I hadn't done at the ranch. My parents didn't care that I had started my own business or that it had nothing to do with horses.

Rubbing my fingertips along the scruff on my chin, I looked from my father, to my mother, and then back again. The least amount of time I had to spend there, the better.

"Fine, I'll stay, but on two conditions. Rafa York can have a part-time job here, and you accept that I'm only here for two months."

"No, absolutely not," Mother said. "You've been gone long enough. You never came home during breaks, not even holidays. You can't leave after only two months. When will I see you again?"

"Let him go, Iris." My dad raised his hand as if he was directing traffic. "That's exactly why he doesn't want to stay. Two months is good enough for me. You can learn a lot in that amount of time. You'll be managing the stables here. I have some good people working for me and they'll show you the ropes."

"Fine, I'll start tomorrow," I said.

I yanked open the door and a pretty blonde girl tripped forward. My instincts kicked in and quickly caught her before she landed on the floor.

She had curves in all the right places and fit in my arms perfectly. As I steadied her, my hand brushed against her soft skin. *Hmm...maybe staying for a couple of months isn't such a bad idea.*

"You should watch where you're going, sweetheart. I might not always be around to catch you," I said.

"My name isn't sweetheart, and the last thing I need is for you to catch me," she said.

"If you say so, but that's not how it looked to me."

I felt her eyes on me as I walked away. I always loved a good challenge and she would be a great one.

***

I never realized how much one person could change everything. Being with Tara made my life worth something, and the time we spent together meant more to me anything. But I couldn't stay at the ranch anymore. And despite how many times I asked her to go with me, she refused.

I postponed my trip to Germany until October, more than six months after Tara and I had met. She never said anything to me about my leaving, but she didn't have to. It was all over her face, in her sad eyes, and on her tear-stained cheek. It broke my heart to leave her, but I convinced myself it was only for a short time.

I spent my time in Germany focused on business. I learned what I needed to and when the day was over, I went to my hotel room and tried to reach Tara. But every night gave me the same result.

"Abernathy Ranch."

I didn't recognize the woman's voice on the other end of the line, but it wasn't uncommon for my mother to bring in new help.

"This is Mason Abernathy. Connect me to Tara Murphy. She's in the stables."

"I'm sorry Mr. Abernathy, but I'm unable to reach her."

The line went dead before I could speak.

"Goddammit," I roared as I threw a glass of water across the room.

Every night there was less time between my asking for Tara and the voice saying she was unable to reach her. I knew something was going on, but I couldn't figure it out. I wasn't sure who I could trust at the ranch so I called the only person I thought might know something.

"Chloe, it's Mason."

"Well hello, stranger," she said. "Been a long time. Where are you?"

"Germany. I've been here almost a month. I'm sorry, I didn't call to be sociable. I was wondering if Rafa has said anything about the ranch lately."

"Rafa? I don't think he's been to the ranch all week." Her voice lowered to a whisper. "He's pretty upset. I think he was fired."

"Fired? That's impossible."

"Maybe I'm wrong. I don't know what happened, but he refuses to talk about it. One night I overheard him on the phone saying something about a bitch."

My mother. I hated that that was the first thing that popped into my mind when I heard that word.

"I'm sorry to hear about that. I'll talk to my father about it."

"How's your girlfriend? I'm surprised she didn't tell you about Rafa."

"I haven't spoken to her."

"What? Why not?"

"It's the time difference. I've been calling her at the ranch, but someone new is answering the phones and won't put Tara on the phone."

"Then call her at home," she said.

"By the time she gets home and takes care of her parents, it's so late out here that I've passed out.

I hate being so far away. Hopefully this business moves quickly so I can get back to her."

"Have you tried calling the personal line?"

"You know my mother answers that."

"And?"

I sighed. "I just don't want to deal with her."

"Well, you know this is just me, but if the guy I loved went away and then never called me, I'd be really pissed."

"I know. You're right."

"I'm always right," she said with a laugh.

"Sorry to cut this short, but I'm going to see if I can get Tara before she leaves work."

"Go! We can talk any time."

I hung up the phone and immediately dialed the private Abernathy line. While my mother was the last person I wanted to speak to, she might be my only chance.

"Abernathy residence."

"Hello, Mother."

"Ahh, Mason. I can't remember the last time you called this number."

She was baiting me into an argument. I needed to stay focused and not let her get the better of me.

"I've been trying to get a hold of Tara."

"I saw Chloe with her parents at brunch at the country club the other day. She's looking lovely. I really think you should take her out sometime."

"Mother, you know she and I are just friends, nothing more."

"I think you'd make a good couple. You're both from the same background and--"

"Mother, can you get Tara for me?"

"Tara? Oh her." Disappointment dripped from her voice. "I thought you'd get that out of your system by now. It's time you settled down."

"I want to settle down with Tara. Can you put her on?"

"You and Tara are from two different worlds. Chloe is really more your type. She can trace her ancestry back for generations."

"Good for Chloe, but she will never be my type. Really, Mother, I never ask you for anything. Can you just do this one thing for me? Get Tara on the phone."

"Well, now you're just being rude. If you want to talk to Tara then you shouldn't be calling the private line."

"I know, but I've tried the main number several times and--"

The line went dead. I threw the phone against the wall as I gritted my teeth. I had to try to get a hold of Tara. I didn't want to think about what she might be thinking. I had to hope that she knew how much I loved her.

Present Day

At night, with the curtains drawn, every hotel room looked the same regardless of the location. They're all boxes with furniture, no soul, no life. It was the little things that differentiated the places. The balcony view for example, or the listing of local restaurants. People thought traveling was fun and staying in hotels was great, but they've never done it like I have.

For fifteen years I had wandered, hotel to hotel, a vagabond billionaire. The only thing that distinguished each place were the people I helped along the way. I saw it all the time, people down on their luck, willing to do anything to make ends meet. Part of it might have been my own loneliness, but helping to get them back on their feet made me feel like maybe my roaming wasn't for nothing.

I opened the drapes and let the sun spill into the main room. I had stayed at this hotel often and slept in this suite far too many times to count. It wasn't home to me and for the first time in a long while, I thought I wanted one.

Home meant a lot of different things to me. Home was in North Carolina where I grew up. It was with my father and mother. More importantly, it was with Tara. I knew that deep in my heart, but I was still angry with myself for giving up.

Sliding my cell phone out of my pocket, I tapped on my father's number. If I had to point to one good thing that happened in the past fifteen years, it was that my father and I became close. I wasn't sure if it had anything to do with my mother leaving him, but with her gone, he became a new man.

"Mason, I was just thinking about you," Dad said. "Where are you now?"

"I'm still in Canyon Cove."

"I spoke to that new assistant of yours. She's a bit of a spitfire, isn't she?"

"Yes, she certainly has a mind of her own."

"Any chance that you and she...?"

"No, Dad, it's not like that at all."

"No? Is she cute? You know I could use an assistant. If you know what I mean."

"You are a dirty old man. You're old enough to be her grandfather," I said laughing.

"So? Look at Hugh Hefner." He laughed until he began to wheeze softly. "Seriously though, all you do is work. It's no wonder you never got married, you never had time to meet anyone. For a while I thought that girl who worked here was it. What was her name again?"

"Tara."

"Yes, Tara. I really liked her. Shame you let her get away. What happened between the two of you?"

"I left for Germany."

"And?" he asked.

"And nothing. I never came back."

No matter how many times I admitted it, saying those words never got easier. I sat on the couch and opened my laptop. As it booted up, the property I took Tara to appeared on the screen. It was still something I was considering. Canyon Cove was the perfect place to move Abernathy Ranch to.

But there was more than just that. I realized that nothing would be a real home to me unless Tara was there, too.

"Mason" Dad asked. "You still there?"

"Yes, I'm still here."

"You still love her, don't you?"

"I do, but it's more than that. I found her. She's living here in Canyon Cove. Somehow life brought us back together again, but all I can think about is the time we lost."

"Then what are you doing yapping away with me? Son, not everyone gets a second chance at happiness."

"I'm not sure she feels the same way," I said.

"Then go and remind her."

Chapter Seven

Tara

After tossing and turning all night, I got up early and went straight to work. No matter what I did, I couldn't stop thinking about Mason. I couldn't ignore how I felt about him anymore. There was no doubt that I still loved him. I probably never stopped.

I pulled my hair back into a low ponytail as I entered the stable. My favorite horse, a chestnut, snorted and nodded his head towards me.

"You're right, honey," I said to the stallion. "We need to go for a ride. The fresh air will do us both good."

I saddled up the horse and rode him past the training area and through the fields to the tree line. As we followed a path through the trees, we reached a clearing that looked out at the rolling hills.

The sun rose higher and gave the hills a golden glow as it cut through the chill of the morning air. Beneath me, the horse snorted again and stomped one of his hooves.

"You're thinking about him too, aren't you?" I said as I patted the side of his neck. "Yes, I know you haven't met him, but trust me, you'd love him too."

I turned the horse back towards the field. There was no point in getting some air if I was going to keep thinking about Mason. I might as well get to work.

As I dismounted, the sun reflected off something and caught my eye. I repositioned myself and noticed it was coming from the hayloft. One of the stablehands took the horse's reins from me.

"Take care of him, I need to check on something," I said.

I yanked down the fold-up stairs that gave us access to the barn's upper level. It was an area we rarely used, so I was curious what could be up there. As I climbed the steps, I noticed a couple of blankets and an empty bottle of wine. I smiled to myself as I let my memories take me back.

Fifteen Years Ago

After we got back from the Kentucky Derby, our relationship grew. We had always spent a lot of time together, but now things were different. I didn't know if he felt it too, but somewhere along the way I had fallen in love with the man just a few months earlier I swore I hated.

The setting sun cast shadows through the stables. Maddie and I were in the tack room cleaning up like we always did at the end of the day. Mason walked out of his office, tipped his hat towards me, and I smiled then looked down at the saddle I was polishing.

"I saw that," Maddie said.

"Saw what?" I asked.

"That look. Those looks I should say." She grinned at me. "You didn't think I was blind, did you?"

"I don't know what you're talking about."

"Oh please, you are so into him. And I think he's into you too. You never told me about the Derby."

"It was just like you'd imagine it to be." I said, shrugging.

"You know that's not what I was asking about."

"Well in that case, you know I don't kiss and tell."

"Do you do other stuff and tell?"

"Shh! You never know who's around," I said, stretching my neck into the barn.

"Like who? You just went away with his family."

"I don't think his mother likes me."

"Iris Abernathy doesn't like anyone. I wouldn't worry about her, Mason has always been his own person."

"If you say so," I said hesitantly. "I just can't help but think she'd do just about anything to get rid of me."

"You're just being paranoid. That's what you get for sleeping with your boss."

"I'm not sleeping with him," I said, unable to stop myself from smiling.

"You see, right there. Thank you very much! That was all the answer I needed," Maddie said with a laugh. "I'm just glad to see you so happy."

"I am happy."

A loud crash made us jump. We ran out of the tack room and into the stable and found Rafa pinned to the ground by a large bale of hay.

"Are you okay?" I asked.

Maddie and I pushed the bale off him and he stood up, brushing himself off.

"How the hell do you get the hay up there?" he said, pointing to the hayloft.

"Oh no, we don't use it for that," I said. "The smaller bales are stored in the back. Those big ones we keep in a separate barn."

"Sorry then, I put some smaller bales up there already. I figured I'd work up to the larger ones. I'll get them down."

As Rafa took a step, he stumbled as his ankle gave way underneath him.

"Oh no, wait. Sit down," Maddie said "You're hurt."

"Nah, I'll be fine. I think it's just sprained."

"You might've broken something. We have to get you to the doctor," she said.

"That's a good idea, Maddie. Take Rafa to the main house and call the doctor. I'll finish cleaning up around here and get those bales down before anyone else gets hurt," I said.

"You sure? Don't you need to get home for your parents?"

"I'll ask Lucy if she can bring them dinner and check on them. Just get him to a doctor."

Rafa leaned on Maddie as they slowly walked down the path to the main house. With my arms folded, I turned and looked up towards the hayloft. I hated going up there.

With my hands on either side of the pull-down stairs, I jiggled them to make sure it was secure. As I climbed the steep stairs, they creaked underneath me. The wood flexed as I stepped on it, making me want to turn around and leave the bales for someone else to take care of.

"You shouldn't be up there by yourself," Mason said as he entered the stable.

I jumped and spun around, almost losing my footing on the steps. Reaching over, I held onto the rickety railing.

"You scared me," I said. "I could've fallen."

"Again, that's why you shouldn't be up there by yourself." He took his suit jacket off and hung it over a stall door. As he folded the long sleeves of his crisp white shirt, he sandwiched me between the steps and himself. "I ran into Maddie and Rafa just now, it's bad enough he's hurt. I don't want you getting hurt too. I'll bring them down." He lifted me off the steps and set me on the ground.

"What are you doing? I don't need your help and I can move from the stairs on my own," I said.

"But you weren't." He climbed up the steps with ease then tossed a bale of hay down. "You wouldn't believe the things that used to happen up here when I was younger."

"Up there?"

"Yeah, my friends used to come over and we'd hide up here and drink, you know, hang out. Wouldn't surprise me if there was still some empty bottles of beer up here."

"Did you bring girls up there?"

Just the thought of him with another girl made me envious. It didn't matter that I didn't even know him back then.

"If I said yes, would you be jealous?" he asked.

I took a deep breath, not wanting to admit the truth, but then I figured why not?

"I know it's stupid, but yes, I would be," I said.

"That's good. I'd be jealous if I heard about you with some guy up here."

He leaned over the edge and looked down at me with a big grin. I couldn't help but think his dimples were mocking me.

"So how many were there?" I asked, folding my arms in front of me.

"How many what? Girls? Hundreds, maybe thousands."

"Thousands, huh? Seems like a lot considering you left when you were eighteen."

"Well, I knew this day would come. I knew one day I would be shoving hay bales down from up here and the woman I loved would be asking how many women I had been with. I needed a lot of practice, you know."

"With thousands of women?" I laughed. "How did you even have time."

"I had to double and triple up sometimes. We had flat-out orgies." He laughed as he tossed down another bale.

"Oh yeah? Orgies? And how old were you when this was happening?"

"I don't know, maybe ten or eleven."

I laughed. "You're such a dork."

"What? You don't believe me? I was quite the ladies man back then."

"Oh yeah, sure I believe you. Just like I believe in Santa Claus."

"What are you talking about? He's real. He still brings me presents."

"I'm sure he does."

He leaned over the edge again. "You know, I always wanted to have a girl up here."

"Just one? Not hundreds or maybe thousands?"

"No, just the one," he said.

The one?

It took me by surprise. Did he mean that or did he say that by accident? Maybe I was hearing things.

"Tara? You still there?"

He leaned over again and as I looked up, our eyes met. My heart jerked in my chest like it did the first time we met.

"I'm right here," I said.

"You okay? You got quiet."

"Oh yeah, I'm fine. I'm great. I was just...umm...thinking about things."

"It's because I said the one, isn't it?"

"Oh? You said that? I didn't notice."

He lay down on the floor and rested his chin on his hand as he looked down at me.

"You noticed," he said. "And I meant it. Now why don't you bring that gorgeous ass of yours up here. I'll show you how much fun it can be."

"I think you're blackmailing me."

"Maybe. But don't you want to come up here? All the bales are gone, it's nice and empty up here. Well, except maybe for a few spiders."

"Spiders? No way. It doesn't matter what you say, there's no way I'm going up there now."

"How about if I told you I love you?"

I stared at him, unable to speak. Did I hear him right? Was he bullshitting me? Would he bullshit me about me that?

"I delayed Germany again," he said. "I have to get out there eventually, but right now there's nothing more important than you."

"But I thought Germany was a limited time thing."

"It is until they find the right investor. I think I'm that guy. They're doing some great progress with new building materials and everything, but honestly I don't want to talk about any of that right now. I just want to talk about you. I love you. And I'm not leaving this loft until you tell me you love me too."

Instead of answering him, I took a deep breath and started climbing the stairs up to him. Mason was standing at the opening at the top, and I focused on him and not the creaking, wobbly steps. He put his hand out to me and I grabbed it quickly, as if I was reaching for a life preserver. His hand made me braver and as I made it up the steps, he pulled me into his arms and pressed his lips against mine.

"Well? Are you ever going to say it?" he asked.

After climbing those stairs, I was woozy and his kiss made me even loopier. I had no idea what he was talking about.

"Hmm? Say what?"

I closed my eyes and pointed my face up, hoping for another kiss.

"Oh, I get it," he said. "You just want me for my body."

My eyes flew up and there were those dimples again, teasing me. I blinked as I forced myself to focus on what he was saying, but all I could think about was falling through the floor.

In the corner, where no one could see us if they entered the stable, Mason spread out some hay, sat down, then patted the ground next to him.

I lowered myself to the floor, careful to not bump my head on the crossbeams from the pitched roof. Worried the loft was going to crack underneath us, I moved slowly. When it didn't even creak, I leaned back on my elbows and relaxed a bit.

"Don't be ridiculous," I said.

"Then why can't you say it?"

"Say that I love you?" I asked. "You know I love you."

"Then if you love me, come to Germany with me," he said. "You know I've been pushing it off so I can stay here with you, but this opportunity is really important to me."

"I know it is. I really don't want to talk about this now though. I don't want to think about you leaving."

"Then go with me."

He leaned closer and cupped my face with his hand. As his lips closed over mine, I leaned back further into the soft hay. I forgot about my fear of the hayloft and about Mason leaving for Germany. I let myself get lost in his kiss.

Mason unbuttoned my shirt and his lips found that spot on my shoulder that always gave me goose bumps.

"Tara?" Maddie called. "Tara? Are you in here?"

I sat up and almost smacked my head against a crossbeam. Mason leaned on his elbow and put his finger up to his lips. Below, I heard Maddie's boots shuffle against the floor.

"Tara?" Maddie said. "Dammit, where is she? Maybe she went home."

As Maddie walked out of the stable, I buttoned my shirt back up.

"I have to get out of here," I whispered.

"No, you don't. She'll be fine. It's the end of the day, you'll see her in the morning."

"What if Maddie sees that my car is still here and comes back? Or what if someone else comes looking for me and they find us up here?"

"You worry too much. Who would they tell? I'm the manager, and I approve of us being here."

"What if they told your mother?"

"Well, there went my hard on," he said. He sighed and turned onto his back and put his hands behind his head. "Alright, get dressed, but you have to promise to meet me here again.

I couldn't help but smile as I pulled my clothes back on.

"Sure, when?" I asked.

"Tomorrow morning at ten. Maddie and Rafa will be training the horses then. No one will be looking for either one of us."

***

The next morning at exactly ten o'clock, I checked the exercise ring and saw Maddie already hard at work. Rafa took the day off to rest his swollen ankle. I quickly walked into the stable and climbed to the hayloft.

Sunflowers greeted me when I reached the top step. Mason stuck them into the clapboard gaps and positioned them into a pathway on the floor. Fresh hay was laid in the spot we were at yesterday. Mason was laying on a thick blanket on top of the makeshift bed.

He stood up and held his hand out to me. I took it and joined him on the blanket.

"You think of everything, don't you?" I said.

"I thought this could be a little fun. You know, a change of scenery instead of my bedroom all the time. Since you've been on the Pill, the possibilities are endless."

"True, but it's not always your bedroom."

"There was that time in my father's library. Several times in the tack room. And of course the sunflower field that day."

"I'll never forget that day. Maybe we should make this another time to remember too," I said as I unbuttoned his shirt.

Leaning forward, he kissed my lips and my entire body melted. I wrapped my arms around his shoulders and shifted myself closer to him.

My hands slid down his muscular chest, to the hem of his fitted shirt, and started to lift it out of his jeans. He yanked it off his body in one swift motion, throwing it off the blanket as his lips found mine again.

I loved being so close to Mason. It wasn't just the sex, it was how he looked at me and touched me. When he held me, I knew how he really felt and what I meant to him.

He unbuttoned my shirt and I lifted myself as it slid down my arms. He smiled at me, making his dimples appear, then moved onto his knees and unzipped my jeans.

The horses' automatic waterer kicked in and startled me. It reminded me of how risky we were being. With the sun streaming in through the windows, my nerves about being naked and getting caught started to get the better of me. I shivered with excitement.

"Every time I undress you, I'm amazed by how beautiful you are," he said, his voice husky and full of passion.

"Stop it," I said, unable to stop myself from giggling as the blood rushed to my cheeks. "I'm already naked, you don't have to kiss my ass."

"Maybe I want to."

He flipped me over onto my stomach and I shrieked with laughter.

"Shhh," he said. "There's people trying to work you know."

He planted his lips on my rump and made a loud smooching sound. I pushed him off and flipped onto my back.

"You're terrible," I said.

He kissed my thigh and slowly his lips made their way up to my hip.

"I'd be more than happy to kiss every inch of you," he said.

I could barely breathe as his lips traveled up my body. My heart raced wildly in my chest and thumped so loudly I couldn't think about anything except where his lips or hands might go next.

Mason dug his fingers into the fabric of my panties and tugged. I lifted my bottom as he slid them off. He kissed my hip again then bit it playfully, leaving me with a mixture of pain and pleasure.

"Stop that!" I said, giggling.

As he gave me his intense brown-eyed stare with a crooked smile, I knew he was thinking of naughty things. He lowered his lips to kiss my stomach, my side, then my breasts as he smiled.

"If I had to choose a favorite part of you, this would be it," he said as he easily unhooked my bra and removed it. "You know, aside from your brain and all that."

"Jerk," I laughed.

His warm tongue passed over my nipples, drawing circles. The surrounding air now felt cold and made them even harder. My body trembled from his touch and as he slowly sucked, my core pulsed. I didn't want him to take his time. I didn't want to get caught. But even more than that, I needed to have him now.

Swiftly unbuttoning his jeans, I slid them down his hips as he moved up and ran his tongue up my shoulder to that sensitive spot again, giving me goose bumps.

With him naked, I let my hands finally have free access to his body. He felt strong, but even though he was muscular, his skin was soft and smooth except for some hair on his chest. I loved the feel of his muscles rippling as our lips met again and we hungrily kissed.

As I shifted my body underneath him, his tongue still slowly moving with mine, his hand slid down the length of my body, then his fingers stroked my inner thigh before he lifted my leg and I felt his manhood pressed against my wetness.

He pulled away from our kiss as our eyes met. My heart raced and my mind spun as I lost myself to the moment. When he slowly entered me, the world seemed suddenly at peace. Everything was perfect. There was nothing more I could ever want and no other place I would rather be.

I wrapped my arms around his back, feeling the long cuts of his muscle and tracing them down his body. Mason's touch intoxicated me, and feeling his cock entering me made the room spin as my body buzzed with approval.

Where we were no longer mattered. All that I cared about was that I was with him. I looked up and our eyes met. His were full of emotion and I knew mine were too.

My body quivered and shook as he shifted his thrusts and rubbed my stiff clit at the same time. Leaning down, he sucked on my shoulder, and that pushed me over. The room spun as waves overtook and shook my body. As I tightened my arms around him, he held me close.

Out of breath, we lay together, our bodies still entwined. I couldn't help but start laughing because everything felt so good, so right.

The sound of the gate on the exercise ring closing brought me back to where we were. Mason kissed my lips quickly then got up to grab our strewn clothing.

"I know," he said. "She's going to be back any minute."

He handed me my clothes and we quickly got dressed.

"That's one bonus for staying in my bedroom," he said. "We can stay there for as long as we want."

Present Day

I left everything in the hayloft just as I had found it. While it had been years since Mason and I had our own secret meetings, I remembered the thrill and excitement of sneaking up there at the ranch. It was our own private hideaway where nothing else mattered except each other. I missed that. Whoever's secret it was that I stumbled upon today was safe with me.

As I pushed the stairs to fold up, I heard the familiar sound of Mason's footsteps coming up behind me.

"If I had known you were going to be up there, I would have come sooner," he said, his voice husky.

"I don't know what you're talking about," I said. "I have always been a lady."

Mason sighed, and I knew his playful side was being tucked away. There was something on his mind.

"I'm tired of this cat and mouse game, Tara. We need to talk. Let's go for a drive."

Hearing those words brought me relief. There was so much that happened in our relationship that I still had questions about. So many things I held onto for so long, both good and bad, and it was time I got some answers. I needed to know why he never came back and no matter how much it might hurt me, I was going to find out.

"Alright, let's go," I said.

Chapter Eight

Tara

Mason and I rode in silence, but I knew it wouldn't be long. As soon as he entered the canyon road, I knew where he was going.

With my hand in his, he kept his eyes on the road. The trip to the clearing on top of the hill felt quicker this time. As we got out of the car, the sun beamed down on us. I squinted and shielded my eyes as I took in the slopes of the hills and the ocean in the distance.

I shifted my gaze and looked at Mason. He was in a suit, minus the tie as I had seen him before. His hair was a little disheveled as if he had been running his fingers through his hair, something I remembered him doing whenever he was nervous. To someone who didn't know him as well, he looked as calm as ever.

On the other hand, I hoped I looked even half as calm. My nerves had gotten the best of me and I found myself alternating between cracking my knuckles and biting my lip. My hands trembled and I shoved them deep into my jeans to hide them.

"Tara, I can't begin to tell you what I felt when I saw you that first time at Xander and Ashley's. After all these years, I never stopped thinking about you or wondering where you were."

I opened my mouth to speak, but he held his hand up. "Please," he said, "just let me get all of this out first. I know what you're going to say. I know it's been fifteen years, I know that I hurt you, just please let's put that aside for a few minutes and hear me out."

He cupped his hands around my face. As his eyes searched mine, I saw sadness in them. I needed closure. I had to find out what really happened, but his eyes made me realize I wasn't the only one who felt pain from it.

"Okay, I'll listen," I said.

Mason took me by the hand and he led me away from the ocean view, back towards the tall trees that framed the other side of the hill.

"I'm going to build Abernathy Ranch here. Right here will be the stables and several other buildings. Everything will be state-of-the-art with the most advanced environmental materials. We'll only take down what we need to to build and leave the rest of nature intact. The top of the hill where we had our picnic will be the house."

"What about your home in North Carolina?" I asked.

"That was my childhood home. I never lived there as an adult. The longest I did was when we were together. And I want that again. There's nothing I want more than for us to be together again."

"What are you saying?"

"I want to build this for us. I want you to move in, Tara. I want our lives to be what they should have been fifteen years ago. I'm building a house, but with you it can be a home."

Fifteen Years Ago

Whenever the ranch was busier than usual, Mason and I would meet in his room. Mason's room was a small building that stood on its own on the other side of the main house. Mason insisted it was the maid's quarters when the house was first built decades ago, but the room was so plain and drafty, I was convinced it was a shed.

Lying in bed with Mason gave me a chance to forget about my responsibilities at home and anything else that was normally on my mind. As I lay in the crook of Mason's arm, he gently rubbed my shoulder.

"I missed you this morning," I said.

He kissed my forehead and held me closer.

"I've been wanting to talk to you about that," he said. "I got a phone call this morning from Deutschland Industries. They're giving me one more chance to come out, otherwise they're selling their shares to another investor."

My heart sank, but I knew the time would come. From the day we met, I knew he wasn't staying at the ranch for long. I took a deep breath and braced myself.

"When do you have to go?"

"They want me there in October."

"October?" My voice rose unexpectedly. I wanted to scream, but that wouldn't help anything. "That's next month. I know you've pushed them off since May, but couldn't they give you more time?"

"I don't think I'm going to go."

"What do you mean? You have to go," I said. "You've been talking about this since we first met. This is a huge deal for you."

"Then you have to come with me, Tara. These past five months have been amazing. We've spent every day together, and I need you there with me. I've never felt the way I feel about you for anyone. I don't want to lose that."

"You want me to go with you to Germany? Are you crazy?"

"No, this is the least crazy idea I've ever had. We've talked about it before, but now you need to make a decision. I want you to come with me."

I was torn. I imagined being in Germany with him, just the two of us together, and it was what I wanted and dreamed about. But I couldn't ignore reality.

"I...I...can't. I want to, but I can't. My parents depend on me. You know I support them."

"I'll take care of them. I'll make sure Brooke has whatever she needs to be there for them. If she needs help, I'll make arrangements for it. I can bring someone in to cook them meals, keep the house clean, whatever they need. You won't have to worry about anything. Just say you'll come with me."

"I...this is just too much. I can't let you do that. I...I just don't know," I said.

"If you don't go, then I'll tell them to go ahead with another investor. I'm not going without you."

"You can't do that. Don't put that on me, Mason. Just don't."

"Then promise me that you'll think about it. That's all I want right now. At least give me that."

"Okay," I said. "I'll think about it."

***

The next few days were a blur. I didn't tell my parents about going with Mason. I didn't tell anyone. No one would understand why I wasn't jumping at the chance to go to Germany with him. I didn't completely understand it either, but I felt a responsibility to stay and care for my parents.

I was freshening some of the hay in the stalls when the strong scent of perfume surrounded me. There was only one person who wore that scent, and I didn't want to see her. I ducked down in the horse stall and hoped she didn't see me.

"Oh, there you are, Tara," Iris said. "I was hoping we could talk."

"Sure," I said as I dusted myself off. I couldn't think of a time that Iris had been out here, but whatever she wanted, I knew it couldn't be good. "Do you want to go into the office?"

"Um no. Here is fine. I just thought we'd have a little chat. You know, just us girls."

She looked around and her nose wrinkled. As I opened the stall door wider, she backed into a dusty wooden post. I tried to not laugh as she looked with disgust at the dirty sleeve of the cardigan she wore over her dress.

"Okay then, let's talk. Just us girls," I said with the widest grin I could muster.

"My son tells me he's leaving for Germany next month."

I could hear Mason's skin being branded with her words 'my son.' It made it harder to like her. Even with how she had always treated me, I wanted to like Mrs. Abernathy and I wanted her to like me too. Despite everything, she was my boyfriend's mother.

"Yes, he is. I'm sure you're going to miss him," I said.

"And what about you? Has he asked you to go with him? Of course I'm grateful he's been around as long as he has and I'm no fool, I know it's because of you."

She looked down her nose at me with more disdain than her dirty sleeve got. I kept on smiling despite how much my cheeks began hurting.

"He did ask me to go with him," I said. "But I haven't decided yet."

"I would imagine it's a lot to think about. But isn't it what you wanted all along? Some rich man to take care of you?"

"No! It's never been like that. I love my job."

"Well then you have a decision to make, don't you? Do you stay here and keep your pride? Or do you go and let everyone you meet think of you as a gold digger?"

"Why would anyone think that?"

"It's what I would think," she said. She pursed her lips as she gave me the once over. "Look at you. Do you really understand what it means to be an Abernathy? You would never fit in. You're just a piece of meat to my son, and that's all anyone will see if you go with him. Look at you." She waved her hand in front of me. "Neither you or your family have anything to offer my son."

The smile was gone from my face. My hands clenched into fists and my heart raced in my chest. I wanted to lunge at her and shove her head into a pile of horse manure. I wanted to scream at her that Mason and I loved each other and what she said wasn't true. But her words cut me to the core and tickled every insecurity I had.

I stood there speechless as she walked into the sunshine. I heard Mason's voice greet his mother as they passed on the path to the main house, but I still couldn't move. I was standing in the same spot, with my mouth hung open in shock, as Mason came and put his arms around me.

"Everything okay?" he asked.

"I...umm...I guess," I said, unable to disguise the confusion in my voice.

"Did something happen? Did my mother say something? I just passed her."

Do I tell him what happened? Or keep it to myself? It was his mother, I couldn't tell him. I wasn't sure myself what even happened, but I knew I felt like I did something wrong. Maybe she was right. Maybe the shame and guilt I felt was because I wasn't right for him.

Going away with him would be too easy. He would support me and my parents while I was away. I couldn't do that. Despite what Iris said, I wasn't a gold digger. If Mason and I were meant to be, then a few months apart wouldn't matter. It was like that song said, if you love someone set them free.

I looked up into Mason's face, and his eyes were wide, waiting for me to say something. I forced myself to look calm and sure of myself, but even as I did that, I felt my eyes begin to fill with tears. Saying the words that had been swirling in my head were going to be the hardest ones I had ever spoken.

"I can't go to Germany with you," I said.

His brow wrinkled, and he looked down at the ground for a moment before meeting my gaze again. I had to force myself to not look away. I set my jaw and swallowed hard as I fought back the tears and tried to look like nothing was wrong.

As his eyes searched my face, I felt my knees begin to weaken. I wanted to collapse. I wanted to run and hide and just let my tears flow. I wanted to cry out with the agony that was filling my chest. Instead I stood strong and waited for him to speak.

"Why?" he asked, his voice full of emotion. "I told you I'd take care of your parents. If it's your job, I can make sure it's still here waiting for you when you get back. Just tell me what it is and I'll take care of it."

"I just can't. I can't."

I shook my head as the tears filled my eyes more. There was no fighting them back anymore. My only hope was that he didn't question anything else because I wasn't sure I could answer.

"Do you love me?" he asked.

I nodded. *Yes, more than anything in the world.* But I couldn't speak the words. Tears fell onto my cheeks and Mason, with a confused look, tenderly wiped them away.

"I wish you could tell me," he said. "I wish I understood why."

I swallowed hard past the knot in my throat. "I'll wait for you. I'll be right here. No matter how long you need to be there, I'll be right here waiting for you."

"I don't want to leave you."

"You have to. You have to go. It won't be long. You said it yourself, a couple of months tops." I forced a smile, but I knew my eyes spoke the truth.

"I'll call you every day, I promise. Even if it's just for a minute, I need to hear your voice."

As he pulled me against him, his one hand went around my back and the fingers of his other hand slipped into my hair. I couldn't hold it together any longer. I lost it. The tears fell fast and I gasped for air. My chest ached from the thought of him leaving. I wrapped my arms around him tightly, digging my fingers into him, not wanting to let go.

***

A month after Mason left and I was fit for the loony bin. Everywhere I looked, I saw him. I heard his boots in the stable. I felt his fingers in my hair.

Each day my heart shattered even more. All I had was my hope that he would call me or come back home. I had no way of getting in touch with him. No way to find out if he was alright.

Well, there was one way, but I hated the thought of it. I didn't want to bother Mr. Abernathy to ask him about Mason, but I figured his mother had to know something. She was his mother after all.

I didn't know if she would tell me the truth. I suspected she was happy that he went without me, even if it meant her son was gone. But I had to find out something. Even if it was just to know that he made it there and was okay.

As I walked up to the main house, I silently argued with myself.

Forget it! Turn around and stay where you belong.

She's his mother, she'll be able to tell you something.

She'll remind you that you aren't good enough to be the gum on his shoe.

Eventually the optimistic me won and I rang the doorbell. I expected Lucy to answer like she usually did, but instead a severe-looking woman with sharp features and her hair pulled tightly back from her face opened the door.

She looked through her glasses, down her nose at me in the same way Iris did. I wrapped my arms around myself and gently squeezed, hugging myself.

"I'd like to speak with Mrs. Abernathy," I said.

"One moment."

I stepped forward to enter the house, but she closed the door. Feeling like an idiot, I stood there staring at the door wondering if I should leave or not. After a few minutes, I turned to walk back to the stables.

"Yes? Oh, it's you, Tara," Iris said as she opened the door.

"Yes ma'am, it's me." I thought about making small talk, but the less time I needed to speak to her, the better. "I was wondering if you've heard from Mason."

She threw her head back and laughed as if I told her the funniest joke. I hated how she made me feel, but I didn't think I had a choice. Iris was his mother, she had to know something. I squeezed my arms tighter to give myself support.

"Of course I have, dear," she said. "What a funny question. I just spoke to my son the other day. He always calls those he cares about. As a matter of fact, he told me he had spoken to Chloe. Do you know Chloe? But of course you don't."

Did he ask about me? Did he say anything about me? When is he coming home?

The questions piled in my head like a multi-collision car crash. I couldn't ask any of them, but with each one, I felt even more wrecked than before.

Why did he call Chloe? Does he still love me? Did he forget about me?

Iris was blathering on, but I couldn't make sense of her words. My mind was racing from anxiety. I was only able to catch some of what she was saying.

"Chloe...beautiful girl...Mason has known her his whole life. Upstanding family...blue bloods like the Abernathys...men sow their wild oats...I'm sure he had a good time."

Each word that registered in my head was like a punch in the gut. I didn't need to hear everything she said, I knew what she was saying. I meant nothing to him. I was just something to bide his time at home, a place he never wanted to be.

I forced myself into the numbness I had spent most of the past month feeling. I had to. I couldn't take his being gone anymore. I refused to think that the past eight months meant nothing to him.

I walked away from her without saying a word. I didn't care if it was rude, she didn't deserve my manners. Most of all I refused to cry in front of her.

My mind spun as it tried to come up with excuses for him. Why didn't he call me? Why didn't he leave a message? The man I knew loved me and cared about how I felt. He didn't want to leave. But the man I knew would have called. Had I been duped all along? Was I just a wild oat?

I stayed at Abernathy Ranch another month before I couldn't take it anymore. I was tired of seeing his ghost wherever I looked. For my own sanity, I had to leave. I needed to move on and not waste any more time waiting for a man who couldn't be bothered to even call.

Present Day

"Tara? Are you okay?" Mason asked.

I looked around the property and could imagine the house, the stables, everything he would build. I could see it as plain as day, but I didn't see me there.

Mason squeezed my hand and I pulled it away. My memories had gotten the better of me. I was in the midst of the pain and sorrow I felt when he left, and I couldn't move beyond that. How could he stand here now when I didn't matter enough for him to even call fifteen years before?

"I can't do this," I said as the numbness I had once grown used to came back. "I can't pretend there was just a hiatus and we can pick it up right back where we started. You left me."

"You told me to leave," he said, his eyes narrowing. "Or did you forget that?"

"I told you I would wait for you. I told you to leave because I thought you'd come back."

"And what did I have to come back to?" he hissed.

"Me! I thought you loved me. I waited for you."

"That's bullshit, Tara, and you know it."

"Take me home," I said.

Mason pointed to his car and we got in, both of us slamming the doors. As he sped off the property, he gritted his teeth as he clenched the steering wheel angrily.

"Did you really think I'd never find out?" he asked. "Did you think I wouldn't hear about him? Is he the real reason you didn't go with me to Germany?"

My eyes widened and my stomach dropped as I turned to look at him. *How did he find out?* I never told anyone about him, not even Maddie.

"Just take me home. I'm done talking to you," I said.

Chapter Nine

Mason

"No, we're not done talking," I said. "For months now all I've heard is about how heartbroken you were. I'm not denying my culpability in that, but you need to admit you were to blame too."

"Me? I was to blame? It was my fault you didn't come back?"

My anger burned deep inside of me. I knew how she felt reliving the past. Since I first saw her I had been reliving it too, but I could keep it in its place. But I couldn't hold my temper back any longer.

"Yes, you are the reason I never went back to North Carolina. You are the reason I never returned home," I growled. "I never went home because I didn't have anything to come back to."

"How long did you think I was going to wait for you to call? I waited months and nothing. You called your mother, you called Chloe, how do you think I felt?"

"You? How do I think you felt? You waited months? Was months how long it took you to announce your engagement?"

I sped onto the long gravel driveway of Jefferson Manor. Glancing over, I saw confusion cover her face.

"Wait, what?" she asked.

"Don't play dumb. I never returned home after I heard you got engaged. I couldn't bear the thought of seeing you with another man." As I pulled up in front of the cottage, the car skidded over the rocks. "You know what, Tara? You were right all along. This was a bad idea."

"Wait," she said as she got out of the car. "I don't know what you're talking about."

"Some things are better left buried."

I drove away before she had the chance to say anything. I didn't want to hear her excuses or lies. Within months of my being away, I heard the news that she had gotten engaged. That was when I stopped trying to reach her. That was when I decided to never return home.

As I reached the canyon road, my cell phone rang. A quick glance told me it was Tara, and I hesitated for a moment before sending the call into voicemail. I was too angry to have a conversation about it. It was in the past, but right now I was reliving it.

My memories of the past flooded my brain. I had my own questions about that time. I had my own hurt to deal with. But deep down I knew that whatever happened between Tara and I was my fault.

If only I had tried harder to reach her while I was away. If only I had pressed her to go away with me. I could get lost in a life of if onlys, but it wouldn't get me what I wanted. The past couldn't be changed.

I tapped a button on my steering wheel, and a chime echoed through the car.

"Call Tricia," I said.

After a few rings, she answered. "Yes, boss."

"I'm going home."

"Home? You mean the hotel?"

"That's exactly the problem. I don't have a home. I've wasted part of my life, and what do I have?"

"A lot of money."

"I'm serious," I said.

"So am I. You got a letter delivered to my house today. You know, the one you said you rented for me and my family. I opened it and it's the deed to the house. You bought it?" she said, her voice full of surprise.

"It's what I do, I'm an investor."

"There's no investment in a house in the middle of suburbia," she said.

"The investment is in you and your brothers and sisters. In your father too. There's nothing more to talk about. When I come back, I'll sign the deed over to you. I'm going home to North Carolina."

"Why did you do this?"

I was quiet while I considered her question. I made investments like this over the years, but not once did anyone ever ask me why.

"Because I like helping people. I think sometimes people run into bad luck and all they need is a helping hand to pull them out of it."

"A job, a house, what you did for my dad, that's all more than just a helping hand. What about you, Mason? Who helps you?"

No one, I thought.

"I don't need help," I said.

"You do. I mean I see how vulnerable you get whenever you talk about Tara. There's a lot there. Things getting better with her?"

"We had a fight. I really don't want to talk about it right now."

"That must've been some fight to make you run all the way home to North Carolina," she said.

"I'm not running. There's just some things I need to take care of out there. It's about time I went back home."

"If you say so, boss. Do you need me to do anything while you're gone?"

"Yes, call Gideon Kohl. He's a local architect and the brother of an acquaintance of mine. Tell him I'm expecting to see a final draft of his plans for the ranch. I'm ready to break ground."

"You got it," she said. "Umm, Mason?"

"Yes?"

"A little advice, don't stay away for too long. I don't know what your fight was about, but if you disappear now, she's just going to think about how you left her in the past."

"I didn't leave her. She told me to go."

"Potato, potahto. You said it yourself she's hurt about you leaving. Don't leave her again."

"Good bye, Tricia."

I ended the call. I wasn't in the mood for logic. It was a perfect reason to head home.

***

I flew stand-by on the next flight. Car service drove me from the airport to Abernathy Ranch. I didn't have any bags, all I had were the clothes on my back.

As I entered the house, my first thought was how everything looked exactly like I remembered. Knowing my father, I went straight to the library where he liked to hide. I was expecting to find him sitting behind his desk, but instead he was doing yoga in the middle of the room.

"Dad?" I said.

"Mason? What are you doing here?" he asked, surprised.

"I'm not sure."

"You look like you need a ride. Let's go, it's my favorite time, just before the sun sets."

We walked out of the house to the stables and everything rushed back. As we entered the stables, my eyes drifted up to the hayloft and I imagined Tara up there waiting for me. The time I spent with her at the ranch was a long time ago, but as long as I lived, I hoped to never forget them. No matter what happened between us.

After mounting the horses, I followed my father down the same path I took Tara on our first date. My memories were as vivid as if it just happened, making me understand Tara's hesitation.

"Have you started building?" he asked as I moved my horse to trot beside his.

"No, not yet. The architect needs to get back to me with some changes I made to the plan."

"What are you going to do about this old place? You kicking me out?" he asked, grinning.

I laughed. "No, you'll fit in just fine. This will become a retirement facility for racehorses. They'll have a place here where they can be cared for without any threat."

"If you're going to be in Canyon Cove, who's going to take care of the place here?"

"The same person who has spent his life here. You. I think I'll start you off cleaning the stables and you can work your way up, learn the ropes."

"You really are a sonofabitch," he said. "Just like your old man."

"How are you and Mother doing living under the same roof?"

"It's like nothing has changed to be honest. She does her thing, I do mine. As long as she's kept in her lifestyle, she doesn't give me any grief."

"I don't get it. If nothing is different, then why get divorced?"

"I felt like I was living a lie, son. I didn't love her anymore. I'm sorry to say that because she is your mother, but it's true. She wasn't the woman I fell in love with. So while she might still be here, I feel different. I'm happy now."

We entered the clearing Tara and I had our first date at and dismounted. While the horses grazed, my father paced the clearing with his hands on his hips.

"Something bothering you?" I asked.

"I was just thinking about how much your mother changed. Maybe I changed too, I don't know." He shoved his hands in his pockets like I often did. "You said you saw Tara? How's she doing?"

"I don't know."

"She's why you're here, isn't it?"

"Maybe. There's just so much in our past together. I just don't know anymore."

"I really thought she was the one for you, son. Maybe she still is."

"I think there's too much hurt there."

"Hurt? Nah, that's water under the bridge. Keep it where it belongs. That's what you build bridges for, Mason. Your road is never going to be smooth, but if you want to get from one place to the next, sometimes you need a bridge or a tunnel or even a damn airplane. The bumps in the road aren't what matters, it's the destination."

"But what if she can't get over it? What if I can't?"

"What's there for you to not get over? She was here waiting for you. She did the right thing by letting you go. The fact that it's taken you fifteen years to come home isn't her fault."

"She wasn't waiting, she got engaged shortly after I left."

"Who told you that? I might be an old man, but I have a pretty sharp mind. I remember that girl was the ghost of herself waiting for you. You have no idea what she went through to leave here. She told me this was her second home and she was right, it was."

"You spoke to her?"

"We kept in touch. When she came to me to hand me her resignation, we had a long talk. I was upset for her. I understood why she left, you gave her no reason to stay. Her heart broke every day she came to work."

"Did she say that?"

"She didn't have to, I saw it. You went to Germany, and lord knows what you were doing out there because you certainly didn't tell us."

My heart broke for her. Hearing how much pain I caused her each day I was gone was the worst thing I could imagine. It was even worse than seeing the disappointment in my father's eyes.

"I did call," I said quietly. "I called her almost every day. I called her here at the ranch. I spoke to Mother, she didn't tell you?"

"No," he grunted. "Doesn't surprise me. She didn't care much for Tara, but that was Iris's fault, not Tara's. Your mother never gave her a chance."

I nodded as I rubbed my beard with my fingertips. I knew then my mother was up to something. But it was still my fault for not trying harder. I assumed Tara would wait for me whether she heard from me or not. I never accounted for her heartache.

"When was the last time you spoke to Tara?" I asked.

"It's been a long time. I haven't heard from her since she moved to Canyon Cove. I don't blame her. I think she was trying to move forward and forget about you once and for all."

My father's words gutted me. How had I been so blind to my mother's conniving ways? How did I not see what I knew was there all along--that Tara loved me as much as I loved her.

I caused her much more pain than I ever realized, and I finally understood what I could do to start making things better.

"Let's ride back," I said. "I need to make a phone call."

Chapter Ten

Tara

"Hurry up, Tara! The movie is going to start."

I looked across the small cottage where Maya bounced excitedly on the couch, a bowl of popcorn on her lap. She waved the remote in the air like a wand.

Since she arrived, we had a Friday night tradition of movie watching and girl talk. We usually stuck to romantic comedy unless we wanted to cry our eyes out, but it was always a great time.

"Do you want whipped cream?" I called out to her.

"Of course, I can't believe you asked. Hot chocolate without whipped cream is like peanut butter without jelly."

"Hey, I like a plain peanut butter sandwich sometimes," I said.

"Mom always said you were weird."

I brought the two mugs of hot chocolate in and set them down on the coffee table.

"How is she doing? I haven't heard from her in weeks. Did she get back from her honeymoon yet?" I asked.

"Uh-huh," she mumbled as she sipped her drink. "Monday I think. I just spoke to her the other day. She's insanely happy."

"That's really great, I'm happy for her."

"And what about you, Aunt Tara? What's going on with Mason? I feel like I've heard about him my entire life and now that he's back in your life, you never talk about him."

"I don't know. I guess things are complicated. It's funny though because when I moved to Canyon Cove five years ago, I swore I didn't need a man. And I meant it. Of course I dated, but not seriously. I don't think I allowed myself to get serious about anyone."

"Why not?" she asked.

"I think something inside of me really believed one day Mason would come back." I sipped my chocolate as I thought. "You know what's funny? About a year after I left the ranch, I started dating again. It was just a way to get out and away from work, to be honest. I was working for a traveling show and while everyone was great, I needed to get away sometimes."

"You joined the circus?" Maya fell over as she laughed.

"No, it wasn't a circus. It was a traveling show with animals and acrobats."

"That's called a circus."

"Whatever, I didn't care. They had horses so I had a job. They were like family."

"Yeah, I can imagine how a bunch of circus freaks would remind you of home."

I tossed a throw pillow at her head. "Remember, you're family too," I said.

"I never said I wasn't a freak." She grinned as she tucked the pillow behind her.

"Well, we'd end up in some cities where the performers had friends, and every so often they'd set me up on a date. There's only so many cities, so I'd come into town and get together with them. It was a nice change from the show to be able to sit at a restaurant and act normal for once."

"Act normal because you were in the circus."

"I wasn't in the circus," I said, laughing. "Drop it already."

"So did you ever have a thing for any of these dates? Or were you just a slut?" She grinned deviously.

"I wasn't a slut." I winged another pillow in her direction and she laughed as she caught it. "They were just dates, two people going out to dinner. I paid my own way a lot so there wasn't any confusion. I had already experienced that once before. Besides, I always told them I was taken."

"Taken? So you lied to them?"

"No, I was setting expectations," I said with a grin. "And I was taken. All that time, even though I had left the ranch and North Carolina, my heart still belonged to Mason. I even remember telling some of them that if Mason ever showed up again that the dates were done and I would go back to him."

"So why didn't you look for him? You knew he wasn't going to be in Germany forever."

"There were a lot of reasons," I said, shrugging. "I did have some pride, you know. But not just that, it was a different time. It's hard to believe, but fifteen years ago, there wasn't all this social media. Not everyone had a cell phone either. Without all those things, how do you find someone you lost?"

She nodded her head slowly, but I could tell her wheels were spinning.

"What about his dad?" she asked. "Didn't you say you stayed in touch with old man Abernathy?"

"I did. But I think we had an unspoken agreement that neither of us would ever mention Mason. He's a very sweet man and perceptive. I never had to tell him how I felt about his son, he just knew."

"He sounds nothing like his wife."

"Well, you know what they say. Opposites attract."

"I still think you should give Mason a chance. You know you still love him."

"I do, but I don't know. Maybe it's not meant to be." I sighed and slouched into the couch. "I feel like there's been so many false starts with him this time. There's so much in the past that I don't know how to move forward in the present."

A throw pillow flew in my direction.

"You know I love you and all, but you're an idiot," she said. "You're not in the present. You're completely living in the past and letting that dictate everything. How many times have you told me about Mason showing up to see you or pushing for you to go out with him? Do you think he's just going to keep coming back?"

"Ouch, Maya."

I turned away from her and took another sip of my hot chocolate as I thought about what she said. Why was I pushing him away? All I ever thought about was him and how much I wanted to be with him again. Was I so hard-headed that I couldn't let the past stay in the past?

"That's what you get with me, tough love and a Sandra Bullock movie."

She turned on the movie, but no matter how much I wanted to get lost in its story, my mind kept going back to Mason. After the way he left last time, I didn't know if there would be another chance. Our last argument was on repeat in my head.

"And what did I have to come back to?" he hissed.

"Me! I thought you loved me. I waited for you."

"That's bullshit, Tara, and you know it."

"Did you really think I'd never find out?" he asked. *"Did you think I wouldn't hear about him?"*

I didn't think he'd ever find out about Jeremy. I didn't know how he found out, but the guilt was killing me. I wasn't just clinging to the past, my shame was very present. How could he forgive me if I couldn't forgive myself?

Fifteen Years Ago

Shortly after Mason left, a new ranch hand came aboard. Usually whenever a new person was hired to work with the horses, part of the interview process was to bring them through the stables to see how they interacted with the horses. Horses were very sensitive animals, and they could tell you more about a person than talking to them.

No one knew where Jeremy came from or who hired him. It was something I would have demanded to know in the past, before Mason. Now I was too busy feeling lost to care.

I didn't care about much and barely knew what I was doing anymore. I didn't bother applying for the job that Mason left vacant even though it was promised to me.

Following routines became my life. It left me no reason to think and the less I had to think, the less I thought about him. I moved in and out of my day like a zombie.

Jeremy seemed more interested in goofing off than doing actual work. He was tall with broad shoulders and shaggy black hair. Maddie and Lucy were crazy about him, but the only time I noticed anything with him was when I had to clean up after him.

It was an unseasonably warm day in November. The stable was suffocating me with its musty air, so I opened up all the doors and brought one of the older horses outside to brush his coat.

Rafa raced over from the other side of the large barn, closer to the main house. He was out of breath when he reached me.

"What's going on? Is everything okay?" I asked, worried.

"The trailer is coming up the drive. The new horse is here," he said.

"Okay, she's a little early, but I asked Jeremy to prepare her stall yesterday."

"And he didn't. Listen, I know the Baylor family. They're real hard asses when it comes to delivering their horses. They came early to deliver a horse at my family's ranch, but we weren't ready. They refused to leave the horse even though it had already been paid for."

"Crap," I mumbled. "Can you stall them? Maybe show them around or something so I have time to prep the stall."

"No problem. I'll grab Maddie and we can double team them."

As I entered the stable, Rafa ran towards the driveway. In the distance, a horse trailer turned in towards the main house. I didn't have a lot of time.

I swept out an empty stall, then grabbed a thick rubber mat and dragged it in place. Using the wheelbarrow, I brought over shavings and was shoveling them into the horse stall when I heard someone walk in. I didn't have time to look up to see who it was. It had to be either Maddie or Rafa letting me know my time was up.

"Are they here?" I asked as I connected the automatic waterer.

"No, we're alone. Finally," said a deep voice.

I spun around and saw Jeremy leaning in the doorway. My first instinct was to yell at him for not getting the stall ready for our new arrival, but then I noticed something in the way he was looking at me that made me feel uncomfortable. I looked down to the other doorway, the one closer to the main house, but no one else was around.

"I'm sure there's some work you can do," I said, then turned back to what I was doing, hoping he would leave.

"I can think of other things I'd like to do."

He cornered me between the wheelbarrow and the water trough. I backed up as much as I could and looked for something to grab to hit him, but nothing was close enough.

"What are you doing?"

"Come on, Tara," he said. "I've seen the way y'all look at me. You especially."

"I don't know what you're talking about."

"You know, that dreamy expression you get."

Did I do that? Had I been so out of it that I didn't even realize I was letting this guy think I was attracted?

"You're dreaming," I said.

His arms closed around me like vise grips, pinning my arms down. As I tried to struggle free, his lips closed down on mine. I jerked back and delivering their horses. They came early to deliver a horse at my family's ranch, but we weren't ready. They refused to leave the horse even though it had already been paid for."

"Crap," I mumbled. "Can you stall them? Maybe show them around or something so I have time to prep the stall."

"No problem. I'll grab Maddie and we can double team them."

As I entered the stable, Rafa ran towards the driveway. In the distance, a horse trailer turned in towards the main house. I didn't have a lot of time.

I swept out an empty stall, then grabbed a thick rubber mat and dragged it in place. Using the wheelbarrow, I brought over shavings and was shoveling them into the horse stall when I heard someone walk in. I didn't have time to look up to see who it was. It had to be either Maddie or Rafa letting me know my time was up.

"Are they here?" I asked as I connected the automatic waterer.

"No, we're alone. Finally," said a deep voice.

I spun around and saw Jeremy leaning in the doorway. My first instinct was to yell at him for not getting the stall ready for our new arrival, but then I noticed something in the way he was looking at me that made me feel uncomfortable. I looked down to the other doorway, the one closer to the main house, but no one else was around.

"I'm sure there's some work you can do," I said, then turned back to what I was doing, hoping he would leave.

"I can think of other things I'd like to do."

He cornered me between the wheelbarrow and the water trough. I backed up as much as I could and looked for something to grab to hit him, but nothing was close enough.

"What are you doing?"

"Come on, Tara," he said. "I've seen the way y'all look at me. You especially."

"I don't know what you're talking about."

"You know, that dreamy expression you get."

Did I do that? Had I been so out of it that I didn't even realize I was letting this guy think I was attracted?

"You're dreaming," I said.

His arms closed around me like vise grips, pinning my arms down. As I tried to struggle free, his lips closed down on mine. I jerked back and smacked my head against the wall. I closed my eyes from the pain.

A metallic thud filled the air. My eyes flew open as Jeremy let go of me and stumbled backwards into the hay.

"Asshole," Rafa muttered, holding a shovel in his hands.

"What's going on here?" Iris said as she entered the stable. In her hands was a camera and behind her were two businessmen I assumed were the Baylors.

What's she doing here, I thought.

"That's it," Jeremy said, rubbing the back of his head. "You can't pay me enough."

He pushed past Rafa and me and walked out. Rafa put the shovel down and ran his fingers through his hair.

"I was just taking care of the trash," he said. "Tara has prepared the stall for our new arrival."

Iris's eyes drilled into me. I felt naked and guilty from her stare. I kept telling myself I had no reason to feel bad, but I did.

One of the men snapped his fingers and Maddie walked in leading a man in jeans and a wide brimmed cowboy hat tugging the reins of a pale horse.

I couldn't stand there with Mason's mother staring at me that way. I must have done something to make Jeremy think I was attracted to him. Why else would he act like that?

The next day, Iris called Rafa for a meeting at the main house and he never came back to work. I wasn't exactly sure what happened, but I had some idea. I took that guilt on as well. Mason brought him to work here to help him get focused on his life and I managed to get him fired.

Everything weighed so heavily on me: Rafa, Jeremy, Mason, that I couldn't stay at Abernathy Ranch anymore. My parents would be fine without me, they had Brooke and Maya now. It was time for me to find somewhere else to go. Some place that didn't have so many memories of Mason.

Present Day

Maya went home shortly after the movie was over. After cleaning up, I went to bed and stared at the ceiling. The sleep I desperately wanted wouldn't come. I couldn't stop thinking about what Mason said to me the last time I saw him. I was to blame.

I never knew what happened to Rafa after that. And seeing Mason after so many years, I was afraid to ask. I didn't want to be reminded of my shame. I had locked it away for all these years. I condemned myself for looking at Jeremy too long, for smiling or saying hi to him too often. Whatever I might have done that triggered those events, I felt guilty about.

The phone on my nightstand started ringing. Since it hardly ever rang, it took me a few seconds to figure out what the sound was. I reached to answer, figuring it was a wrong number.

"Hello?" I said.

"I hope I didn't wake you."

The voice was deep and husky. I recognized it immediately as Mason but just as quickly convinced myself it was someone else.

"No, I was awake."

"Couldn't sleep?"

"I've just been lying here."

"Wish I was there with you. I couldn't sleep either."

I blinked a couple of times and looked at the ceiling again. Was he really on the phone? Now? After all this time?

"I'm surprised you called," I said.

"I should've called sooner."

Yeah, you should have. I bit my tongue to keep from saying what I was thinking.

"I did try calling when I was in Germany," he said. "I tried all the time."

"Then why didn't I know?"

"Because they never told you."

"Who? My parents? My sister?"

"No, my mother and whoever she hired to intercept my calls. I should've called my father, but we weren't close at the time. I didn't think it would make a difference."

I let the words roll over me as I breathed a sigh of relief. Hearing his mother was involved made sense to me. He didn't owe me any explanations. Everything became clear.

"Your mother told me you called her and Chloe. She said you called the people you cared about," I said bitterly, unable to hide it from my voice.

"I knew what she was doing and I let it happen," he said. "I should have tried reaching you at home. Thinking back, I don't know why I didn't. I let everything else get in the way and convinced myself you'd just be there when I came home. I loved you, but I took you for granted."

"But you never came home."

"No, I told you. I heard you got engaged. I was hurt and angry, but I had no right. I wasn't around and you thought I didn't care."

"Wait a second," I said. "You keep saying I got engaged, and I don't know what you're talking about. I've never been engaged. Despite us being over, a part of me was always waiting for you."

"But you looked guilty the other day. I know you, Tara. I know that look. That look told me you were keeping something from me."

I swallowed hard and breathed deeply. Mason was the love of my life. If I wanted things to work with him, I had to tell him everything.

"I...I am guilty," I said. "You're going to think it's stupid, but maybe I flirted with a new ranch hand. And he tried kissing me."

"What do you mean maybe? And if that's it, if that's all there is, then why do you feel guilty?"

I closed my eyes and pulled the pillow over my head. Having to explain it after all these years was so ridiculous. As I tried to put it into words, I realized there was no reason for my shame. Whether I looked at Jeremy a certain way or not, I didn't force him to kiss me. But I still had guilt for what happened after.

"It was my fault that Rafa got fired," I said. "I'm so sorry. I know he was getting into trouble and you brought him to the ranch to help him out, and I ruined all of it."

"Tara, it's alright, it's in the past. Just tell me what happened."

"What do you mean it's alright?"

"One thing at a time. I need to know what happened."

"The new guy Jeremy…tried kissing me. He was a big guy and I just wasn't myself. I didn't expect it and…I just…I couldn't fight him. He had me trapped." I sighed as I remembered Jeremy's arms pinning mine down. "Rafa walked in and hit him with a shovel, but your mother entered the stable shortly after that."

"My mother was in the stable? Did you hire this Jeremy person?"

"No, I didn't take the manager position when you left. I couldn't. It's embarrassing to admit it, but I barely felt functional after you left. None of us knew who hired him."

"My mother," he snorted. "I'm sure it was her. What happened after that?"

"Jeremy quit right there and then. Your mother wanted to speak to Rafa privately and he never came back. I only stayed on for another month before I left too."

"I'm pretty sure I can piece together what happened."

"I felt so bad about Rafa that I kept this a secret. Whenever I would look you up, I'd try to find out about him too, but I could never find anything. Are you still friends with Chloe? Did she ever say anything about him?"

"When I called Chloe from Germany, it was because I couldn't reach you. I called her to find out if she knew what was going on at the ranch. She didn't know what happened, but she suspected that Rafa had been fired by my mother. I didn't want to speak to her, but she was my last hope to reach you so I called and asked her to get you. Of course she didn't."

I finally had the truth. After all these years, the heartache I felt when I thought about Mason leaving was dulled.

"When I came back to the States, I started traveling. I dove into work to keep my mind off of you. There were so many times I thought of trying to find you, but I thought you were happy with someone else and it killed me just thinking about it."

"Sorry," I said.

"It's not your fault. My mother did this," he grumbled. "Rafa was fine after being fired. He finished high school and went on to veterinary school. When my father signed Abernathy Ranch over to me, I hired Rafa on to take care of the horses."

"I'm so happy to hear that," I said. "I was so worried that he'd get into something bad like he was before. I've felt so guilty about what happened for so long."

"You have nothing to feel guilty about. None of that was your fault. If anything, it was my fault. If only--"

"No, just don't even say it. It's all in the past and it's definitely time for us to move forward."

"You know, I never stopped loving you. Not for one second. No matter how mad I was when I thought you had moved on, I still loved you."

"I still love you too," I said. "I never stopped."

Chapter Eleven

Mason

A week had gone by, but I was still at the North Carolina ranch. After all this time, it felt odd being there. It was only exacerbated by my realization that this was my first time back since my father signed the ranch over to me.

My mother had a favorite room in the house where she kept some of her favorite collectibles on display. She kept the door closed and no one was allowed inside. But the room had a beautiful view of the stables, so it had to be mine.

As I stood in the center of the room, the sunlight streamed in through the tall windows. I didn't tell my mother I was having her things packed. She didn't deserve any notice. With everything she had done, she was lucky her things were being packed and not thrown in the trash. I heard the click of her heels on the wood floor in the hall before she appeared in the doorway.

"What is going on here?" she exclaimed.

She grabbed a painting out of a muscular packer's hands. Rushing to another packer, she swiped a delicate vase from him. Her eyes swept over the room until they landed on a stack of sealed boxes.

"Mason, why are they doing this? Tell them to stop."

"No," I said sternly. "I've decided to make this room into my office. You can tell them where to put your boxes or Goodwill will be here to collect them as a donation."

"Why are you doing this to me?" she shrieked.

"Remember Rafa York? Why don't you tell me what happened to him?"

"Rafa? Well, you know what a troubled young man he was. I can't be bothered with remembering the details."

"Charlie?" I said.

"Yes, sir." A packer with his sleeves ripped off and tattoos lining his arms raised his head to look at me.

"Drop the next vase you pick up."

"No!" Mother said, gasping.

"You mean this one?" he said, holding up a blue and white vase that probably belonged in a museum.

I nodded and Charlie let it crash to the floor. The porcelain split into hundreds of different pieces. My mother's mouth dropped open in shock.

"Why did you do that? I don't understand," she said.

"Tell me what happened to Rafa," I said.

"I already told you, I don't know."

"Charlie?"

He picked up another vase and held it with the tips of his fingers at shoulder height.

"No, don't do this," she said. "Okay, I get it. I'll tell you about Rafa."

I held my hand up and Charlie brought the vase closer to him.

"What happened to Rafa, Mother? Remember to choose your words wisely. I want the truth or the vase gets it," I said calmly, raising my eyebrows.

"I saw him forcing Tara to kiss him. I stopped it and then fired him," she said.

"Drop it, Charlie."

The vase clattered to the ground but didn't break. The big man gave it a confused look, then dropped his construction boot onto it. He turned and gave me a huge smile.

"Oh no!" she said, covering her face. "Okay, okay. Please just don't break anything else. I hired a new ranch hand shortly after you left."

Charlie picked up a tall, thin vase with red flowers.

"Continue," I said.

"Rafa found him forcing himself on Tara. They got into fisticuffs and I fired them both."

I turned to the packers. One of them was wrapping a delicate tea set. I took one of the tea cups and dropped it onto the hardwood floor.

"No! What did you do that for? I'm telling you the truth," she said.

"Because you left something out. You are a manipulative, sad person, and I know you had something to do with what happened," I said.

She sighed and yanked the tea pot out of the packer's hands.

"I hired him to woo your girlfriend. He was supposed to sweep her off her feet, but she didn't even notice him. I told him to get pushier with her and Rafa heard the struggle and rescued her. I fired them both." She wrapped her arms around the vase Charlie was holding and pulled it to her. "Now are you happy?"

"You know what, Mother? Rafa was right, you really are a bitch. Charlie, have some fun. Just make sure you clean up afterwards."

As I walked out of the room I heard several items crash to the floor. My mother screamed at Charlie to stop, but he kept going. He had his instructions.

Mother ran out of the room and grabbed my arm to stop me.

"How can you do this to me?" she cried.

"You're crying over objects, Mother. You fucked with me. You tried to hurt the woman I love. And you succeeded in breaking us apart. I lost years of happiness because of you. Because I loved someone you didn't approve of."

"It's not the same. You're doing this on purpose to hurt me. I didn't mean to hurt you."

"What did you think would happen when you told me Tara was happily engaged to another man? Did you think I'd laugh? Maybe I'd smile? Did you ever consider you might be breaking my heart?"

As she stared at me, confusion and fear passed across her face. She never thought about how I felt, it was always about her and getting what she wanted.

"Don't bother answering," I said. "I know you never considered my feelings." I turned and began walking away from her, then turned around to face her once more. "I'm your son!"

She flinched as I roared at her. Then she put out her hand and reached for the sleeve of my jacket. Her fingers touched it gently before she looked up and our eyes met.

"But my things," she said.

"I told you before, you have your boxes. You'd better tell them where to put them before they're donated."

I yanked my arm away from her and walked into my father's library. He was writing in his journal and looked up as I walked in. I closed the door behind me to drown out my mother's cries.

Out the window, I spotted a trainer with his black hair pulled back into a ponytail working with a Thoroughbred in the exercise ring. Based on my father's descriptions, it was Joseph, the man my father had sworn could speak to animals in their own language. Only today, that horse did not want to listen.

The mare bucked Joseph off the saddle and then pranced around the ring. The palomino's coat was a golden color that reminded me of Tara's hair.

I took my suit jacket off and rolled up my sleeves as I went outside. Joseph was standing still, his back straight, as he physically tried to show the horse who was boss.

"New horse?" I called out.

His eyes darted over as I entered the ring.

"Mr. Abernathy?" he asked.

"Call me Mason."

"This is the most stubborn horse I've yet to meet. She won't take a rider no matter what I do."

The horse nodded, her head high as she pranced in circles.

"Looks like she agrees with you," I said. "What's her name?"

"Diva. Fitting, isn't it?" he said with a grin.

"Have you tried running her?"

"How can I? She won't let anyone ride."

The mare stopped and dipped her head over the fence for a drink. I walked closer to her, making sure to let my boots shuffle a little on the ground so I wouldn't startle her. As I leaned against the fence, she turned and looked at me, then went back to drinking as if I wasn't there. When she was done, she whipped her mane and neighed.

Slowly, I approached her and when I was closer, I reached out and rubbed her muzzle. When I stopped, she pushed her head into my chest. I patted her neck, then checked the saddle. I suspected she wanted more than just trotting around the ring.

"Come on now, Diva," I whispered. "Don't let me make a fool of myself here." I grabbed her reins and looked over at the practice track. "Open the south gate."

"I mean no disrespect, but she'll run."

"Just do it."

Just beyond the gate was the empty track. Diva's ears flickered as she watched Joseph open the ring.

"You want to race, don't you?" I whispered.

Diva kicked at the dirt with her front hoof. She kept an eye on me as I tugged on her saddle, then patted her neck. With one swift motion, I put my boot into the stirrup and mounted the saddle. She shook her head and backed up, but I leaned down towards her and whispered.

"Let's race."

She galloped out of the ring and I led her onto the track. After a full turn, I tugged on the reins to slow her down and brought her to where Joseph was waiting. He shook his head as he grabbed her bridle.

"You're going to make me lose my reputation here, Mason," he said with a laugh.

"I guess she just likes me."

I dismounted and patted Diva.

"Still, you won her over. I've tried everything. I was ready to give up."

Until last week, giving up was what I was ready to do with Tara. I thought about the months I had been trying to win her back. Nothing I did mattered. I couldn't flatter her, I couldn't bribe her, I was at the point where I almost gave up on a relationship with her. In the end, it seemed so simple though.

Diva had racing in her veins, it was all she cared about. Tara just wanted the one thing I had promised to do all those years ago.

"Tell me, Mason. What's your secret? How did you win her over?"

"I called," I said.

"Huh?"

Grinning, I handed Joseph the reins. He was a smart man, he'd figure out how to handle Diva eventually. I was stupid with how I tried to handle Tara. I thought she would give in to whatever I wanted because we still had feelings for each other. I ignored how she felt about the past because I didn't want to remember it.

The past week I spent every night talking on the phone with Tara. It was something I should've pushed myself to do years ago, but I was just as stubborn as that horse. I thought Tara would know how I felt and what I was thinking without my saying so.

As I walked away, I watched Joseph mount Diva's saddle. As they trotted around the track, I knew it was time for me to really go home. Not home where my family was, but home to my heart.

I entered the house and walked back to my father's library. The door was open and my father was still seated behind his desk. As I walked into the room, he looked up at me.

"You're leaving now, aren't you?" he said as he slipped his glasses off and set them on the desk.

"Yes, but I promise I'll visit more."

He smiled as he nodded slowly. "More than once every fifteen years would be nice."

"Once the new ranch is complete, you're more than welcome to stay with me."

"I'm looking forward to it, son. And I have a feeling that the next time you make the offer, it'll be an us."

I stepped around to the other side of the desk and hugged my father. He patted my back, then stepped away.

"Enough of this sappy crap. Go catch your plane and get me my future daughter-in-law."

Part Two
A Chance to Forget

Chapter Twelve

Tara

The bell above the door chimed as I entered Mirabella's. I waved to Amy, who was behind the pastry counter, and looked around the crowded restaurant for my friends.

Cassie's hand shot up and waved to me to come over. She was Ashley's cousin and practically her twin with her wavy dark hair and bee-stung lips. Seated next to her was Becca, her old roommate. Becca's light brown hair was pulled into a messy bun that showed off her freckles. Beside her was Samantha, who left her curly red hair loose.

Samantha was the reason we started meeting at Mirabella's in the first place. She was an in-demand caterer and was always looking for new restaurants to try.

"Where is everyone?" I asked as I got to the table. "It's not like Ashley to miss our get-togethers."

"She just texted me that she can't make it," Samantha said. "The baby has a slight fever. She said he's fine, but she couldn't leave. I don't blame her. I'd stay home too if I was her."

"And I just heard back from Deborah," Cassie said. "She thinks she's coming down with something. I bet she has a case of Mr. Sexy. She never gets sick." She laughed as she put her phone away.

"Has anyone heard from Jackie?" I asked.

"No," Samantha said. "I've texted her several times, but she hasn't gotten back to me. I hope she's okay, this isn't like her."

"I'd love to keep waiting, but I need to order lunch," Becca said. "I have to get back to work."

"I'm starved, so I definitely think we should order," Samantha said. "But since you brought up work, anything new with that hot man you're working with?"

"Hot man?" Becca asked.

"She means Gideon," Cassie said. "He's been all over lately. He's really making a name for himself in the architect world."

"Gideon? Yeah, I guess he's hot, but we're just friends. I don't see him as anything else."

"We'll see," Cassie said as Amy came to take our orders.

As we finished our meals, the doorbell chimed. Becca waved her hand and we turned to see who was walking into the restaurant. Jackie entered, looking disheveled. Her make up was smeared and her clothing was a little wrinkled. As she ran to our table, she smoothed her hands over her dark hair, but her hair wouldn't lay flat.

"I'm sorry I'm late," she said.

"What's going on with your hair?" I asked, trying to not laugh.

"Nothing," Jackie said. "I just...I overslept. I have bed head."

"That looks like sex hair to me," Becca said with a giggle. "Who is he?"

"Who? What? No one of course. You know I'm not interested in dating anyone."

As she sat down beside me, I noticed her shirt wasn't buttoned properly.

"Jackie, where did you learn how to button?" I asked.

Jackie looked down at her blouse and as she realized what was wrong, her face turned beet red.

"I was in a rush," she said, forcing a smile.

"Who is he? Is it Brent? I bet it is," Samantha said with a satisfied smile. "I'm telling you, you're made for each other."

"We hate each other. You know that."

"Hate is a powerful emotion, just like love."

Jackie rolled her eyes then shook her head.

"No. Just no. Get it out of your mind, Sam. You're just trying to get us together because you want us to be sisters-in-law."

"Yes, I do. The last thing I want is some bitch I need to hang around with," she said with a laugh. "Honestly though, I really do think you'd be great together."

"Do you ladies need anything else?" Amy asked as she walked over.

"Unless Jackie wants anything, I guess we'll take the check," I said.

"It's already taken care of," she said.

"What do you mean?"

She widened her brown eyes as they met mine and then her eyes darted towards the door. I followed her gaze to the glass doors and spotted Mason standing outside.

Deja vu.

"You should've told me he was here," I said.

"He just got here, but he made me promise I wouldn't tell," Amy said. "Besides, that's not who paid. You ladies have men fighting for your check. Someone beat Mason to it."

"Who?"

Amy's forehead wrinkled as she thought. She flipped her notepad open and looked through several pages of orders.

"I wrote it down. I knew I'd forget," she said. "Brad...no...Bram...no..."

"Brent? Oh please Amy, say it was Brent," Samantha said as she bounced in her chair excitedly.

"Yes, that's it," Amy said. "Brent. Umm... Winslow if I remember correctly. He even overpaid so you could get whatever you want."

"Oohh, Jackie, you are definitely keeping something from us," Becca said.

"No, there's nothing. I told you, we can't stand each other. He probably just did it because we had a fight at your dinner party the other night."

"You did? You didn't tell me that," Samantha said.

"This isn't the first time. All we do is fight," Jackie said. "Anyway, there's nothing to talk about there. Unlike with Tara." She turned to face me with an expectant grin. "What's Mason doing here? Or did I miss the update?"

"Yeah, Tara," Cassie said. "I didn't want to ask just in case your dates ended up being bad news. I can't believe you didn't tell us."

I looked out to the front of the restaurant and noticed Mason was wearing jeans instead of a suit. It took everything in me to stay in my seat and not run out to see him.

"I know you," I said. "If I told you what happened, I'd never hear the end of it."

"Just tell us already," Samantha said. "Jackie's not going to give us any juicy details so you're in the hot seat."

"Okay, okay." Like a criminal who was caught, I raised my hands up in front of me as they laughed. "You know what I was going through, thinking about the past and how I couldn't get past it. Well, it ends up I wasn't the only one. Mason had been just as lost all these years."

"But how did he win you back?" Cassie asked. "The last time we spoke, you said you couldn't get past the hurt and he was trying to act like your being apart didn't happen."

"He called me," I said with a shrug. "With our having nothing but the phone between us, we were finally able to talk. For the past week we've talked every night for hours. Sometimes we even talk during the day too. We got everything out in the open where it belonged. Ends up it was all a big misunderstanding created by his lovely mother."

"Ha, no surprise there," Cassie said. "All I ever hear about are these terrible mothers-in-law."

"I love mine," Samantha said. "You see, Jackie, there's another reason to marry Brent."

"Marry him? Are we back on that again?" Jackie said, throwing her hands up in the air.

While Samantha began planning another dinner for Jackie and Brent to spend time together at, I gave my friends a small wave and left the restaurant. As I stepped outside, I saw Mason had moved further up the sidewalk and was deep in conversation. He was speaking with a handsome blond man with a strong jawline and a dimple in his chin. He was so striking I thought he looked like he had stepped out of a movie.

"You should come by this afternoon," Mason said. "Gideon will be there and he can discuss all the plans. I'm telling you, you'll never see a more environmentally safe construction. We're keeping as much of the land as intact as possible. And the materials we're using are cutting edge. Most of the ranch will run completely on solar power."

I gently touched Mason's back to let him know I was there. He turned around and put his arm around me before kissing my lips and smiling.

"Tara Murphy, this is Brent Winslow. We just ran into each other. He owns the largest environmental protection firm in the nation."

"It's nice to meet you," I said.

As Brent held his hand out for me to shake, his sleeve peeked out of his jacket. I couldn't help but notice his cuff was unbuttoned. It reminded me of Jackie and her bed head and I laughed to myself.

"Likewise, Miss Murphy," Brent said. He pulled his hand away quickly and tugged on his sleeve until his cuff disappeared. "Mason, I'm definitely interested in seeing what you have going on there. I have a meeting downtown, but I'll pass by a little later."

As Brent walked away, Mason turned to face me and pulled me closer to him.

"What are you doing here?" I asked. "I thought you were still in North Carolina."

"I wanted to surprise you. Come with me. Let's go for a ride."

With his arm around me, he led me to his car and opened the door. We had talked so much on the phone recently that I felt that closeness again. The years we had been apart didn't mean anything anymore. I was ready to pick up where we left off.

Chapter Thirteen

Mason

I planned on seeing Tara as soon as I arrived back in Canyon Cove, but due to my delayed flight, I went directly to the hotel. I paced my hotel room and looked at the time, annoyed it was so late. While I was disappointed, nothing was going to stop me from talking to her on the phone. In just a week, we had fixed the problems from the past and were moving forward. To say I was happy to have Tara back in my life was an understatement.

I slipped my Bluetooth headset into my ear and sat on the couch. As her phone rang, I waited anxiously to hear her voice.

"Well hello there, stranger," she said.

It always amazed me how much she still sounded like a Southerner even though she had been away for so many years.

"Hey gorgeous," I said. "I hope it's not too late."

"I thought maybe you forgot about me."

"I could never forget about you. I just had some last-minute things to take care of. What are you doing tomorrow?"

"Tomorrow is lunch at Mirabella's with the girls."

"You can't cancel?"

"No, they'd string me up if I did. Besides, I love getting together with them. I'm looking forward to it. Why?"

"Maybe I was thinking I'd take you out for lunch."

"Well, you're a little far away."

For a moment I thought about telling her I was close and could be at her place in less than half an hour, but I stopped myself. She loved her time with her friends. I wasn't going to make her choose between us.

"I won't be far for long," I said.

"I'm looking forward to that. I miss you."

"I miss you too. So, are you in bed already?"

"I was just falling asleep when you called," she said with a small yawn.

"Oh? What are you wearing?"

***

As I drove the car out of the city and towards the canyon, I glanced over at Tara. For the first time since I had seen her again, she looked calm and relaxed, like the Tara I remembered.

"You have something on your mind," she said.

"I do. But I'm not sure if I should say anything about it yet."

She nodded slowly then looked out the window. I had a feeling she knew what was on my mind. She knew where I was taking her and that I wanted her to move in.

"Then maybe you should wait," she said. "Wait for when the time is right."

"Time is fleeting. And waiting is what kept us apart."

"Then say it."

I didn't. As I turned onto the property and saw how many construction vehicles and people there were, I knew it would have to wait. I wanted to do it when it was just us, Tara and I.

In the week I had been gone, they broke ground on the main house and the horse facilities. Tricia visited daily and sent me photos of the progress while I was away, but the pictures didn't convey how massive a project it was until I saw it in person.

Tara and I walked up the hill towards the center of activity, where the house would one day stand. The foundation had already been poured and framing had begun. Tricia was talking to some of the workmen when she spotted us and came over.

"You must be Tara," she said with a big smile. "I'm Tricia, Mason's assistant."

"My condolences," Tara said with a laugh. "I would not want to work for him."

"He didn't give me much of a choice," Tricia said.

"That's enough," I said. "I should have kept you two apart longer."

"Well, it's nice to meet you, Tricia. Mason told me a lot about you," Tara said.

"That's a relief. I was worried you wouldn't like me."

"What's to not like?"

"You know how we met," Tricia said. "I'm sure some women would have a problem with that."

Tara shook her head as she smiled. "Not with Mason. I know him too well."

I slipped my arm around Tara's waist. I loved feeling her soft curves against me.

"Come with me, I want to show you around the house," I said.

"You do realize there is no house?" she asked.

"Use your imagination."

As I brought Tara to the framed section where the front door would be, Gideon Kohl, my architect, stopped us. He was in his mid-twenties, the age I started dating Tara. But he was much cockier than I ever was.

"Now hold on," he said. "You can't go in there without a hard hat."

Gideon's gaze dropped to Tara. He tilted his head to the side and grinned at her as he removed his hard hat and his sandy blond hair fell onto his forehead. I knew his look. Every man knew that look.

"Well hello there," he said to Tara. "I'm Gideon. If I knew there was going to be a beautiful woman here today, I would have dressed better."

He tugged on his fitted button-down shirt, then rolled up his sleeves a little more while flexing his biceps. I balled my hand into a fist, ready to pummel him. Tara put her hand on my chest to stop me.

"I think your mommy dressed you just fine," Tara said.

Gideon burst with laughter. "Woot! I love a feisty woman." His phone started ringing and he turned from us to answer. "You're back at work? No, I told you I was going to be on site today. How about dinner tonight?" He hung up, reached for two hard hats, and handed them to us.

"Girlfriend or wife?" Tara asked.

"Huh? What? Oh no, nothing like that. We're just friends," he said.

"Sounded like a girlfriend to me," Tara said with a knowing look.

We put on the hard hats and I took her through the skeletal house towards the area we had our picnic at. She leaned towards me and whispered.

"Becca was just talking about her friend Gideon at lunch," she said. "You can't tell me there's more than one Gideon in Canyon Cove who's also an architect."

"There's definitely more there than just friends," I said. "You know we were friends first."

"No, we weren't. You even said our first date happened on the day we met."

"I didn't say we were friends for long," I said, cocking my head to the side like Gideon did.

"I've been doing a lot of thinking about the past. I was young and dumb back then," she said.

"And what about now?"

"Now, well I'd like to think I'm not dumb anymore, but lately I think I have been."

"No, I'm the dumb one. I expected you to go back to the way you were just because it was what I wanted. That wasn't right."

"You did it because you were upset about the past. I get it now. I was too stubborn to before," she said as she looked towards the ocean. "What's going to be here?"

"It's a courtyard off the master suite. When I had Gideon design it, I told him it had to be here. I said I wanted an area where you could sip your hot chocolate and look at the ocean."

She tilted her head up towards me, her nose wrinkled like it did when she was confused. I knew she was expecting me to ask her to move in again, but I wasn't going to. Not now and not here.

"Remember our trip to find the Menorquín horse?" I asked.

"How could I forget?"

"Then what would you say if I told you I have a plane leaving tomorrow for Spain?"

"But it's late in the year. Isn't it going to be chilly?"

"Then I'll keep you warm. I've done it before," he said.

"What am I doing thinking about the weather?" she muttered. "Ask me again."

"What would you say if I told you I have a plane leaving tomorrow for Spain?"

"I'd ask what time you're picking me up."

He kissed me and I knew that everything was going to be alright. Being with Mason was what I always wanted. It was the one constant in my life where I didn't have any doubt.

Chapter Fourteen

Tara

"Feels like just yesterday I was here in the cottage asking you about Mason," Ashley said as she stirred another marshmallow into her hot chocolate. "And now he's whisking you away."

"And he's building a house for her," Maya said as she joined us at the round dining table.

"He is not building a house for me, he's moving the main ranch to Canyon Cove," I said.

"Did he ask you to move in?"

"Yes, but he chose to build it here. I had nothing to do with that."

"You're crazy if you think that's true," Ashley said. "I think you're playing dumb with us."

I shrugged. I wasn't ready to tell them everything that happened. I hadn't told anyone everything about the picnic or our late night talks, I wanted them to stay just mine for a little longer.

"You can't tell me he chose Canyon Cove out of the blue," Maya said.

"I think he chose it for the scenery," I said.

I had given up trying to sound convincing.

"If you say so. I'm just wondering when I can move in here." Maya looked around the room. "You won't be needing any of this furniture, right?"

"Oh, so that's it, you just want the cottage. You're kicking me out," I said as Maya laughed.

"No, it has nothing to do with you, I just like the scenery," she said.

"Are you packed yet?" Ashley asked.

"Yes, but I have to admit I'm a little nervous. It's been so long since..." I raised my eyebrows and gave a small shrug.

"Since you did it? Trust me, I don't think that's changed," Maya said.

"Is that all you think about?" I asked.

"Since I've been single, yes."

"Well, that's not what I meant. I'm just nervous because I feel like so much is riding on this trip. The last time we were there, we became a couple. This time we're going as a couple. I know I'm overthinking it."

"I don't think you have any reason to be nervous," Maya said. "He loooooves you."

Maya started making kissing noises and I rolled my eyes.

"You are just like your mother," I said laughing.

"I'll take that as a compliment."

"You two are something else," Ashley said. "Did you say he's taking you to Spain?"

"Yup, to the Balearic Islands. He wants to make up for the time we went there."

"Balearic Islands?" Maya asked. "That's like Ibiza, right? Joshua has been trying to convince me to go there with him. You've heard of House of Argenti, right? You know, the big fashion house."

"The big everything," Ashley said. "I've heard Luca Argenti is always looking for more sophisticated and elegant ideas."

"Well, Joshua said House of Argenti is hosting this huge invitation-only weekend bash there. He has some ideas that he thinks would be perfect for House of Argenti. He's just waiting to see if he would get the invite," Maya said.

"You should go if he does," Ashley said. "Joshua is a great friend. The two of you could drool over eye candy together on the beach."

Maya shrugged and her face saddened.

"I don't know that I'm ready for that," she said.

"I think some time away from here would be a good thing, Maya," I said. "Some fresh air might help you get him out of your mind."

"Speaking of Ibiza, Tara," Ashley said, taking the pressure off Maya. "I thought you said you weren't dating when you and Mason went there before."

"We weren't. That trip was complicated, but that's when we became a couple. He promised me then he'd take me back one day."

"Because you didn't do the deed," Maya said, snorting as she laughed.

"You're impossible," I said.

"I think Maya's right," Ashley said.

"Well, there are worse ways to spend my time. If that's all this trip ends up being, you won't find me complaining," I said with a grin.

***

Mason and I had been in Spain for four days and hadn't left the yacht once. We sailed around Ibiza, Mallorca, and Menorca in the beautiful blue water. The days were sunny and warm, but the nights were cold.

After so many days, we needed to restock the ship so we docked in Mallorca. The water was unlike anything I had ever seen. In some areas it was a dark blue, in others almost teal.

We promised each other we wouldn't bring any work clothes with us so Mason left his suits at home, instead opting for jeans. I left my jeans at home and chose comfortable cargo pants.

We strolled from the port to the white sandy beaches. It was my favorite kind of beach day, cool enough that it was empty except for the diehard sun worshippers. Mason helped me climb a rocky hill that followed the coast line back to the port. Once we reached the top, Mason turned to me, his expression serious.

He squinted in the sunlight as I waited for him to say something. He had something on his mind and after we had been so open with each other, I was wondering what he was keeping from me now.

"What? Stop staring at me like that," I said. "Did something happen? Do we have to go back? Seriously, Mason, if you don't speak right now I'm going to have a fit."

His eyes twinkled as he grinned.

"Nice to see I still drive you crazy," he said.

"You've always driven me crazy."

"And I always will."

He reached behind him and pulled a long, thin box out of his back pocket. He looked at the box for a while and then back at me before he spoke.

"We've been together a long time and even when we were apart, I thought about the day I could give you something that showed me how much you mean to me," he said.

He looked at the smooth box hesitantly as he balanced it between his fingers. I wanted to grab the box from him and open it to see what was inside. Mason had never looked so nervous before.

"What is it? What's in the box?" I asked. "I'm sure no matter what it is, I'll love it."

My mind raced as I thought of the things that could be in the box. A small voice told me that it was most likely jewelry, and I groaned inwardly. Not that I didn't love jewelry, but I wasn't the kind of person who wore much. That fancy stuff wasn't something I really cared about.

"Tara, I had this idea to give you this, but Tricia and even Ashley told me it was a bad idea. Until this second I was confident in what my gift is, but now I'm not so sure."

He handed the box to me and I was surprised at how light it felt in my hands. I opened the hinged top slowly as I tried to peek inside, but all I saw was an envelope. I took the envelope and Mason removed the box from my hands.

"Open it," he said.

The envelope was thick and as I broke the seal, I found the rounded edges of paper folded into thirds. I flattened the forms and read the cover page.

This document conveys ownership of Lucky Lady Diva, Standardbred Mare of Abernathy Ranch, to Tara Murphy.

My jaw dropped as I read the words over and over. Tears sprung to my eyes as I flipped the pages and read about her lineage and saw photos of my horse. My horse. Not someone else's. I hadn't felt this excited about a gift since my eighteenth birthday when my parents gave me Ladyfinger.

"Are you serious?" I exclaimed.

"You've spent all these years caring for other people's horses, I thought it was time you had one of your own. She's a Palomino and has quite the personality. I think the two of you were made for each other."

"This is the most incredible gift, Mason. You did good."

"I knew I did, but at the last minute I had doubts."

As the sun began to set, we made our way back to the yacht. We lay down together on an oversized lounge at the rear of the ship while the driver steered out of the marina. Mason was quiet again. I knew he had something on his mind.

"What's bothering you?" I asked.

"I was just thinking," he said. "I've traveled the world and I've seen a lot of things, but I only have one regret in life."

"What is it?"

"That I never asked you to marry me before I left for Germany." He shook his head as his brows drew together. "I was stupid. I thought you knew how I felt and that would be enough for you."

"There's no point in this, Mason. The past is in the past. What's important now is that we're together and whatever problems we had have been solved."

"You're right, but I'm thinking about the future now. I know I've asked you before and I made a lot of presumptions about us, but that house I'm building in Canyon Cove? That entire ranch is for you. No matter how many times you say no to me, it doesn't matter. I will keep building it and I will wait for you to change your mind."

I was wondering when he would bring it up again and I was surprised he hadn't mentioned it before. I expected Mason to ask me when he showed me around the property the other day and now that we were together with nothing to get in the way, I kept waiting for him to ask me again. I wanted him to ask me again. I was ready for it this time.

"You sound very sure of yourself," I said.

"That's how confident I am in our feelings for each other. I've never been more sure about anything in my life than when I think about a future with you."

"Then ask me."

He sat up, a brow cocked at me in mild surprise.

"Come live with me and be my Love," he said.

I laughed. "Now ask me without quoting Shakespeare."

"That's Marlowe," he said, his eyes twinkling.

"Well, you know some people say they're the same people."

"You're changing the subject," he said.

"Then ask me like a normal person."

"Will you move in with me?"

"You live in a hotel, why would I move in there?"

"Tara..." he scolded.

"I know, I know. There's a time for jokes and now isn't one of them. I can't help it."

"I know you can't. It's what you do when you're nervous. But you have no reason to be nervous with me."

"I know I don't. Being with you is the easiest thing I've ever done. Of course I'll move in with you. I love you," I said.

"I love you too. Always," he said.

Five Months Later
March

The shrieks of wild parrots flying overhead woke me. I opened my eyes and tried to focus on the alarm clock. Whatever time it was, it was too early. I rolled over to check on Mason, but he wasn't there. He usually woke before I did, but never this early.

The glass wall facing the courtyard was open, explaining why I was awakened. I reached for the button to close it, then noticed sunflowers on my lounge chair.

I stepped outside and noticed the calming ocean in the distance. The sun was just beginning to rise, making the sky colorful.

"Since I'm already awake, I might as well watch the sunrise," I grumbled.

Curling up on the chair, I admired the flowers for a moment and thought back to the day we met.

"I was hoping you'd wake," Mason said as he entered the courtyard. In his hand was my favorite mug, a purple mug with a cranky Tinkerbell on it that said 'mornings aren't magical!' "I bought you some hot chocolate."

"You have some nerve waking me up so early," I said as I took the mug from him. "I was looking forward to sleeping in."

"Maybe tomorrow, darling. Today is special."

"Anything special can wait until I'm awake."

"There are a lot of things I can do to wake you up," he said as he kissed my neck.

I yawned and gently pushed him away. "Not now. I have morning breath and morning everything."

"I love your everything no matter what time of day it is. You always look beautiful to me."

"Now I know you're just kissing my ass. What's going on?" I laughed.

Mason sat on the edge of the lounge chair, facing me. He cocked his head to the side and grinned, deepening his dimples and reminding me of the first time we met. I might have been falling through the door, but when I thought back, that was the moment he swept me off my feet.

"Do you know what today is?" he asked.

"Hmm." I pretended to be deep in thought, but I knew what the date was. How could I forget it? "St. Patrick's Day?"

"You know that's next week. We're having dinner with Ashley and Xander," he said. "You give up?"

"Yup, I give up. I have no idea what today could be."

He eyed me suspiciously for a moment.

"I don't believe you, but I'll tell you anyway. Sixteen years ago today you fell into my arms for the first time."

"Has it really been that long?"

"I think that was the moment I fell for you," he said.

"Now I know you're lying. You don't believe in love at first sight. Plus I was the one who fell. Literally."

"It wasn't first sight," he said. "I held you in my arms and that was it for me. I actually think hearing you call me an asshole was what cinched the deal."

"You really are one, you know?" I playfully swatted him with a sunflower. "I couldn't stand the thought of you. You were so smug and confident."

"I think you've used the word cocky to describe me."

"Yes, you are the definition of that word."

"You didn't like me, yet somehow you kept falling into my arms."

"I'm a klutz. Don't confuse that with my swooning over you."

"You were my damsel in distress. You're lucky I was always around."

"I'm lucky you're still around," I said. "I'm still very klutzy, you know."

"Since you didn't remember today is the anniversary of our meeting, I'm sure you don't remember what I told you on our first date."

"Which first date? The actual date or the one you like to pretend was a date? You know, I've been thinking, and I can see an argument for our trip to Spain as our first date."

"Spain was our second date. I'm talking about the one I know was our first date. I made a promise to you out in the clearing that day." He lowered himself to one knee. "I told you one day I'd marry you."

Mason brought a small jewelry box out of his pocket and held it in his hand. He opened it, but I didn't see what was inside. I couldn't tear my eyes away from his.

"Will you marry me?"

"I'm not sure," I said.

He snapped the lid closed and stared at me blankly.

"What do you mean you're not sure?"

"Well, I've been thinking about what you said, and basically it's taken you sixteen years to propose to me. I think you're settling." I tried to hold back my laughter.

"I'm serious, Tara. In all of this time that we were apart, I had only one regret. And that was that I didn't ask you to marry me when I had the chance. When I ran into you that day at Jefferson Manor, I knew I was being given my second chance. There was no way I was going to waste it. And even that didn't turn out as planned."

"No, it didn't because you acted like Mr. Alpha Male Caveman."

"What can I say? Seeing you made me think with something other than my brain."

"I know. I'm just teasing you, Mason."

"You were always a ball buster," he said with a laugh. "Besides, I figured since I waited sixteen years to propose, maybe we could wait another sixteen to get married."

"I hate you," I said as I swatted him with a flower again.

"Does that mean you're saying yes?"

"That means I'll pencil you in in sixteen years."

"Pencil?"

"Yes, in case I need to erase. I have to keep my options open in case someone else comes along."

"That's no way to talk to your fiancé."

"Fiancé? I never said yes," I said.

"The caveman in me isn't taking no for an answer."

He picked me up from my seat and carried me back into our bedroom. He dumped me on the bed and lay back, facing me with his head on his hand, his elbow on the bed. He rested the ring box inches away.

"Hey, not fair!" I said between laughs. "I'm still weighing my options."

"Whether you marry me or not, you know we'll be together for the rest of our lives."

"I do. I even knew that when we were apart. I always knew some day we would get back together again. That's why being away from you hurt so much."

We lay on the bed together and he leaned forward. His lips closed over mine as his tongue slipped into my mouth. I forgot about how early it was, I even forgot about my morning breath. All that mattered was that we were together. I didn't need someone to tell me something I felt deep down inside.

The piece of paper didn't matter to me, but I knew it mattered to him. I grabbed the box and opened it. Inside was a simple diamond solitaire. I slipped it on my finger and Mason pulled me closer and kissed me.

"I promise you I'll spend the rest of our lives making up for the time we lost," Mason said. "I love you and I don't want you to ever question that."

"No more promises. Just being here with you every day is enough. Even if sometimes you're a cocky asshole."

"I'm a cocky asshole who has always loved you and will always love you," he said.

"I love you too."

I didn't know when we would get married, but knowing Mason, he would want to do it soon. As I closed my eyes, his lips moved along my body as he removed my nightshirt. I imagined a small wedding at our home with our friends and family. The thought made me smile and with it, any pain that I held on to from the past finally vanished.

As he held me, I wrapped my arms tightly around him, grateful to have him beside me after all this time. It saddened me to think that his mother had caused so much pain, but the past didn't matter anymore. What mattered was that despite everything, we never stopped loving each other. I had always called Mason the love of my life, and now I knew I was his too.

About The Author

Liliana Rhodes is a New York Times and USA Today Bestselling Author who writes Contemporary and Paranormal Romance. Blessed with an overactive imagination, she is always writing and plotting her next stories. She enjoys movies, reading, photography, and listening to music. After growing up in New Jersey, Liliana now lives in California with her husband, son, two dogs who are treated better than some people, and two parrots who plan to take over the world.

Connect Online

www.LilianaRhodes.com

www.facebook.com/AuthorLilianaRhodes

Made in the USA
Middletown, DE
21 June 2018